SWEET CHAMPAGNE

A Silver Fox Resort Novel

LYZ KELLEY
ANN STUART

About the Book

All these years she's loved him, and now fate is asking her to decide. Try one more time or walk away.

Paige Weaver hasn't been home to California since the tragic death of her beloved older sister, a loss that ripped her family apart. Sixteen years working overseas as an English teacher has done little to heal her grief or diminish her unrequited love for Noah Myers, her sister's high school love and widowed husband. When Noah calls and invites Paige to attend a family wedding as his plus-one, she tries her hardest to resist the lure of reconnecting with Noah and the tight-knit circle of friends and family who once meant so much to her. At a crossroads in her life and desperate to make peace with her past, Paige finally accepts Noah's invitation.

Running away is what Noah Myers does best—from grief, from commitment, and, fastest of all, from memories. Like his sister-in-law, Paige, he abandoned everything familiar after cancer claimed his beautiful young wife. Noah's heart still bears the scars of loss, and guilt about being unable to save her still haunts his days and nights. After reluctantly agreeing to attend his little sister's wedding, Noah reaches out to the one person who's always been there for him, the very special woman who seems to understand his feelings without him saying a single word. But instead of revisiting unwanted memories, Noah's family reunion begins the healing process and triggers an astonishing insight.

From award-winning and best-selling author Lyz Kelley, comes Paige and Noah's second chance love story about their search for happiness after years of heartache from avoiding the one person destined to be their true love.

Note from the Author

One of the things I enjoyed most about writing Paige and Noah's story was exploring the dynamics of a large family. Although he hasn't been home in many years, Noah values his relationships with his mother, siblings, nieces and nephews, and cousins. His sister's wedding is the perfect occasion for Noah to reconnect with family...and finally confront his past.

Let me introduce you to the Myers family and friends. If you have trouble with names or keeping track of who's who, this handy cast of characters will help. Siblings are listed from oldest to youngest.

Dolores and Lance Weaver, parents to

- Olivia Weaver (deceased)
- Paige Weaver (an integral part of the Meyers family history, but separated from them since her big sister Olivia's death)

Bernice and Henry Myers, parents to

- Julie (married to Brent Keyning), parents of Charlotte (Charley), Ben,
- Kaylee (married to John Westhouse), parents of Luke, James, Riley, Emma, and Max
- Logan (divorced from Cindy), parents of Reece and Ethan
- Noah (married to Olivia, who died of cancer at age 24)
- Mia (engaged to Alec Stark)

**Rosa Myers (Henry's sister),
and assorted cousins**

Chapter 1

ey, how about being my plus-one for Mia's wedding?

Paige Weaver choked off a gasp while re-reading the message on her phone.

Noah Myer's lighthearted invitation to be his date for his younger sister's wedding forced her to concentrate on breathing.

He didn't really want a date.

At least not in the true sense of wanting a relationship. He wanted a shield. Someone to protect and deflect his loving yet interfering family from setting him up on a designer date —a mom and siblings who didn't understand why a member of the Myers family couldn't settle into a more conventional lifestyle.

She'd anticipated this call, which was why she'd done her best to avoid the wedding topic and his bemoaning texts all week.

If she hadn't been expecting a call from one of her Vietnamese students about a private English lesson, she wouldn't have answered without seeing who it was, and wouldn't now be staring at her phone, unsure what to say or do about Noah Myers, the one guy all others were measured against.

Her secret crush since childhood, he'd always been a splinter in her thumb. But he would forever be off-limits because he'd unfortunately met and married her older sister first.

Things might have turned out differently if Noah hadn't discovered Olivia was dying, because Noah and Olivia were as opposite as left and right. They never agreed on anything, had no similar hobbies, they didn't even like the same kinds of movies. But Noah and his valiant heart had been determined to save Olivia, even though the doctors quoted him the standard three-percent survival rate for her type of cancer.

In Noah's eyes, Olivia was pure sunshine, and nothing bad could touch her. At twenty, he was determined to beat those quoted odds. But the cancer proved him wrong, and that failure forever destroyed his faith in love.

Come to California. It'll be fun!

She groaned, closed her eyes, and pictured Noah graphic designing away on his laptop in some out-of-the-way café in Singapore, earbuds muting the noise of the crowd coming and going around him, his phone flung carelessly next to a cup of *kopi*. His work as a digital nomad—doing graphic and website design and social media for companies—was a perfect career choice. Perfect, because the job allowed him to travel around the world, never staying in any place long enough to get attached to anyone or anything. Over the past sixteen months he'd lived in Bali, Portugal, Malaysia and a half-dozen other places, and the past several months in Singapore.

Like her, he fled California after Olivia lost her battle.

In the span of six short months, Paige had lost her sister

and best friend, and her parents withdrew into their grief, going their separate ways.

The only glimmer of light was when a family friend invited her on a trip to Prague. When the three-week summer vacation was up, she elected to stay, get a work visa, and escape from the insanity of her life and the consuming grief she was doing her best to ignore.

Noah, in his smothering grief, wasn't helping her heal. She needed space. Time. But he found her eventually. After all, who else would understand the pain he suffered?

Paige reread his text, calculating ways to avoid answering his direct question.

She typed out: *I've got lots going on here. Not sure I have the time.*

She watched the three dots flash until his response appeared. *Please tell me you aren't skipping. Mia told me you haven't RSVP'd yet.*

That was true enough. Paige glanced at the thick ivory vellum invitation leaning against the fruit bowl on the counter between the tiny kitchen area and the living room. Even though Mia was marrying the love of her life at a luxurious resort on the California coast north of San Francisco, Paige had no intention of putting her heart through what was sure to be a weekend of painful memories.

Not because Mia and she weren't good friends, but because acquaintances from the old neighborhood would also be there. There would be awkward questions, sad looks, and comments about how nice it would have been if Olivia could be there as well.

Olivia. Olivia. Olivia. Paige blew out a frustrated breath. Everything was always about Olivia.

For years after Olivia was diagnosed, Paige's life had been about arranging schedules around doctors' appointments, cancer fundraisers and hospital stays. If she could have traded places with her sister, she would have, but life was cruel, so instead Paige ended up fading into the background until she was invisible, even to this day. She hardly heard from her dad, and her mom only called when she needed something. Otherwise the conversations were too awkward.

Paige was tired of being invisible—at least to the ones she loved.

And even though she didn't plan to return home, she hadn't been able to bring herself to tick the NO box and send the response card back. Refusing the invitation to avoid confronting her past was cowardly, but attending Mia's wedding would force Paige to face people, places, and feelings she said a final farewell to years ago.

Sorry. My schedule's been crazy busy, she texted back, evading his question once again.

The muscles in her chest tightened as more bouncing dots appeared on the screen.

I'm flying in early. Got a website-building gig at the resort where the wedding is being held. Mia wants some family time before the wedding chaos. Come. You can hang out with us. Say you're my date, and I'll cover your ticket. Please. Bail me out. Mom's putting on the pressure.

Paige sighed and shook her head. *So your mom is putting on the grandbaby pressure again. Gotcha.*

Her finger hovered over the keypad, torn between wanting to say yes and knowing her answer had to be no.

She'd never be able to keep her feelings neutral while both of them were in the same place at the same time. She wanted so much more than a just-friends relationship, and clearly Noah was blind to her desires.

Then again, Noah only dated women who were emotionally unavailable. He had a habit of wining and dining a woman for a week or two before sending her packing with some vague excuse or other. Paige might have considered him a jerk if she didn't understand the deep-seated hurt behind his playboy persona. Of all the people in the world, she was one of the few who could empathize with his pain— a pain which had kept her running on a parallel track for the same amount of time.

I'll pass, she typed, then hit send, because saying yes to Noah Myers would hurt too much. *Ask one of your ex-girlfriends to go.* She hit send again as her heart and mind played tug-of-war.

Her heart was already envisioning long walks on the beach at sunset, maybe a candlelit dinner for two, slow dancing to the sound of waves rolling onto the beach.

The phone buzzed with a new text.

And subject an ex-girlfriend to my family? No thanks. Besides, Mia wants you there.

Mia, but not you, her practical mind added to the text even though it wasn't written.

Paige shivered as a breeze from the open balcony door wafted in, along with the racket of honking cars and revving motor scooters from the street below. She glanced out her window at the familiar sight of building rooftops. If she stood, she'd be able to see all the way to the river, busy with boats and cargo ships floating by.

She missed California's expansive, tree-filled parks and people picnicking on blankets, taking a walk, or sitting on a bench reading. And then there were the bike paths where a person could safely explore the city. And the quiet cafés where a person could daydream for hours.

What am I doing?

Don't give in to him.

Don't you dare give in.

She glanced again at Noah's message, regret punctuating each heartbeat as she punched in her response.

How about we schedule a group call, she texted. *That way I can catch up with everyone.* Her offer was a compromise, even though she'd have loved to visit The Silver Fox Resort, which Mia gushed over when they chatted on the phone a few weeks back.

Her cell rang, and Noah's name popped up on the screen. Her thumb hovered over the answer button. So typical of him to keep pushing. Noah could be stubborn as a mule when he wanted something.

She sighed, then swiped to accept the call and steeled herself to hear the voice she still heard whisper in her ear, night after night, in her dreams. "Hello, Noah. It's still a no. I need to figure out what I'm doing next semester, and that means job hunting."

"Mia will never forgive you."

His deep baritone triggered a longing that started in her belly and rose up to pierce her heart. Just the sound of his voice was enough to open the floodgates of bittersweet memories, prayers that a miracle cure would save her sister, and the envy she still tried so hard not to feel.

"Stop right there, Noah. Mia won't hold a grudge. She's forgiven me for worse. She'll be upset, but she'll understand."

"Your summer break begins in, what? Two, three weeks?"

Paige moaned, and he chuckled.

"Meet me in California. Your friends miss you. I miss you. My family misses you. It'll be fun."

Oh, no. He was doing it again. She swore he'd be able to convince a rock to roll sideways.

"Noah, please don't add to the pressure. I have a lot of things I really do need to do here."

"Like what? Whatever it is can't be more important than Mia's wedding."

Oh, he sure knew where to poke to get the right response.

How could she admit to him that, at thirty-four, she was

lost? Without a plan, without a compass. Unable to let go of the past to grab the future.

She was sick and tired of moving to a different country every couple of years, but without the distraction of a new job, new students, and a new culture to explore, she could end up either staring back over her shoulder at a past full of pain and secrets, or facing forward into an empty, loveless future.

She had built a great career, had interesting friends from every corner of the globe, and she was debt-free, with a tidy sum in the bank. But the years had folded into one another, and she'd come to realize none of those things eased the lingering pain. They only masked it.

If she was honest with herself, she was still the lost, lonely eighteen-year-old who wanted her family back, and stubbornly stayed in Europe out of a bitter longing for what could never be again. How ironic that Olivia's death had also obliterated Paige's hopes and dreams.

She wanted a home, a husband, children. A place to belong. Someone to build a life with, to put down roots with. Noah had been and still was the man she loved. But he would never be hers. His heart belonged to Olivia, now and forever.

"I need to…take some courses to keep my TEFL current. My Teaching English as a Foreign Language program waives continuing-ed if I earn additional certifications."

"I thought once you had your teaching certificate you were good to go."

"Not if I want a better paying job, or any teaching job in the States."

"You're moving back?"

"Whoa there, buddy. I mean *if* I move back. I love teaching in Vietnam. The culture here is rich, people are friendly. But more and more young teachers are coming in each year, and since their salaries are lower than mine, they get more hours."

Besides, sixteen years of living a transient lifestyle was weighing her down, not lifting her up as it once did. It was time to go—but where? She rose from the loveseat and padded over to the balcony, scanning the cityscape as if the answers might be hiding among the high-rises and blocks of apartments.

"There must be online classes. You can study once you get here. Better yet, you can look for a job. Come on. When's the last time you were back in the States? Ten, fifteen years ago?"

"Actually, I haven't been back, at least physically anyway. I've been on lots of video calls with friends."

"Wow? Not at all?"

She shook her head. "Nope. And don't talk to me about taking a class. You know I won't be able to study once I arrive. With your family, there won't be a minute to spare. There'll be food to cook, games to play, last-minute wedding preparations. It'll be pure chaos. It always is with your crew."

She blinked against the burn at the back of her eyes.

Growing up, she'd adored her visits to the Myers' home. With five kids, the household was always in an uproar, but it was the best kind of commotion. Lively teasing, unbridled laughter, reassuring hugs, and Mrs. Myers' world-famous oatmeal raisin cookies.

"You want to say yes. So just say yes." His voice dropped to a husky whisper. "What's holding you back?"

She couldn't tell him the truth, so she did what she always did to avoid questions she didn't want to answer. She responded with a question of her own. "Why do you need me at the wedding? You could ask a dozen other women."

Paige held her breath, hoping he might finally see her as an attractive, intelligent woman, not as his sister-in-law or the little sister of his high-school sweetheart.

"I don't want the hassle of taking someone I barely know to the wedding. That would be messy and complicated. My whole family is going to be there, and they already know you. Come on. Meet me in California."

She sighed, not hearing the answer she'd hoped for, but he did know her, and so did his family. During the months before Olivia's death, his sisters, brother, and parents were at the house most days to help with dishes, laundry, or any other small chore.

"I don't know, Noah."

"Come on, Paige. You can relax, hang out, enjoy the beach. And if you want, you can beat my sisters at cards again. It'll be great."

Relaxing did sound nice, and being around family sounded even lovelier.

Every day, her life was all go-go-go. Every weekend, she would pick up extra shifts to teach English to the parents of her students. In her down time, she went on day trips or holiday excursions with friends.

The lure of several days at an exclusive coastal resort with Noah and people she'd once been close to was too much to resist. If she tried, just a tiny-weeny bit, she could imagine herself in a lounge chair by the pool with no worries. In the spa, having a massage. Going hiking. Eating organic meals that weren't cooked in fish oil. Ah, it was tempting.

And then there would be Noah.

She could create new memories, even if it was just as friends, instead of always imagining him with Olivia—taking her to chemo appointments or holding her hand or making her smile as she lay in bed dying. She owed him so much for making Olivia's last few months special. Guilt about saying no to Noah began to sting.

But not as much as her grief, because Olivia took the

heart of the one man Paige ever truly loved with her when she died.

"Did I mention the offer comes with a plane ticket?"

"All right, all right! I'll go with you, but only as friends. Does that change your offer?"

Paige's disgruntled acceptance earned a chuckle.

"Not at all. I'll email you the flight details shortly. See you in a few weeks."

Noah disconnected before she could say more. She slouched against the balcony doorframe, a little dizzy with a welter of emotions.

She was going to see Noah. And even though she tried, she couldn't squelch the thrill making her skin prickle.

The traffic noise, shouts in Vietnamese, and aromas from cooking stalls rose up to her second-floor studio apartment, but she closed her eyes and transported herself back in time to life in California with Olivia, her parents, Mia…and Noah.

But Olivia was gone. She and Noah were still alive.

Her lids fluttered open, and reality sank in.

She was going home.

She glanced at the miniature carved rock collection sitting on her television stand, and then the handmade pottery dishes she loved. She could pack those up with the few other belongings she intended to keep and leave them with a friend until she figured things out. The studio apartment was furnished, so she just had her clothing, jewelry, family photos, and personal items.

She took a deep breath. Yes, it was time to leave.

And even more important, it was time to face her past, her sister's death, and her feelings for Noah. The last being the hardest of all.

Chapter 2

*P*aige accepted his offer.

Noah leaned back from his home office desk and linked his fingers behind his head, a satisfied tingle working its way up to his hands.

His family, specifically his two older sisters, had been pressuring him for weeks about who he was bringing to the wedding. Last week he told them he had a plus-one to get them off his back but hadn't yet given them a name.

He'd considered taking Jess, but hopes for a lasting relationship faded when she demanded he take her drinking and dancing for the third night in a row. Those demands, plus her request to stop communicating with his "female friend," sealed the door shut. Wild nights and jealousy weren't on his list of wants. At forty, he wanted a life partner, not a dance partner. He wanted a woman with depth and intelligence, one who had big dreams but enjoyed the small pleasures. He knew what love and commitment were like… and Jess wasn't it.

Yet, showing up without a date meant nonstop nudges

toward any single woman within a five-mile radius—not how he wanted to spend his visit.

Thank goodness for Paige.

Thoughts of her acceptance made him smile—that, and the last picture she sent, showing her zip-lining through the jungle. Paige had always been active and energetic and athletic. The opposite of Olivia, who was a girly-girl, totally into fashion and makeup. Despite their difference in age and temperament, Paige adored Olivia and vice versa. Neither ever uttered a negative word about the other.

A faint ding sounded, and Noah leaned forward to accept an incoming video call.

"Hey, Mia. You're up early. It's not even daybreak in LA." He checked his watch, calculating the time in California.

"I'm a busy bride. No time for sleeping in. I've been up every morning for the past two weeks by six a.m. Why should today be any different?" She yawned and took a careful sip of her steaming coffee. "Am I interrupting anything?"

"Nope. I couldn't concentrate, so I shut down early." He considered asking if Mia knew why Paige hadn't accepted the wedding invite, but figured asking would open the door into his personal life, which he did his best to keep firmly closed. His sisters were rather opinionated when it came to his lifestyle, and he'd rather they keep their ideas to themselves.

Yet, it still bothered him that Paige hadn't accepted. She and Mia were practically inseparable growing up. Both competed in soccer, ran track, and studied more than most of his friends did. Some might have wondered why Paige didn't go to college like Mia had, but he knew the reason.

But the reason Paige didn't want to attend Mia's wedding eluded him.

Maybe she'd tell him once they were together.

Replaying the conversation, he recalled hearing her voice —hesitant and a little breathy at first, relaxed and playful by the time she agreed to attend with him—brought back memories.

Good memories.

Sad memories.

Precious memories.

He didn't know what would have happened if he hadn't had Paige to talk with during those first few years after Olivia passed. The days were bleak. He was confused and lost, and he spent most of his days working construction, trying to wring out the anger swamping him. During the long nights, Paige was the voice on the other end of the line.

His connection to life.

The voice of reason.

He'd always be thankful for her friendship and how she'd help pull him out of the darkness.

"Hey, listen." Mia lifted a sheet of paper, one corner visible on the display. "I'm just finishing up the seating chart, and I need to know who you're bringing to the wedding so the calligrapher can finish the place cards. You've been talking about this Jess person like there was some potential there. Mom wants to meet her."

"Yeah, well. Things didn't work out." Noah grimaced in response to Mia's raised eyebrows and cynical frown.

"What happened this time?" Mia asked. "Too young? Too old? Didn't want to follow you on your jaunts around the world? Had her own itinerary? Beauty but no brains?"

He shrugged. "It just wasn't a good fit. Let's leave it at that."

"Not a good fit as in not into a Double-D? You're a boob man, right?"

"Mia…" he warned.

She laughed. Leave it to his sister to know all the right buttons to push.

"So, are you coming alone? If you are, no worries. I have plenty of single friends attending. Those who remember you from when we were young would love a chance to get reacquainted. Most of them had secret crushes on you." Mia took another slug of coffee, her early-morning bleariness fading with every sip, but he could see the snicker she was hiding behind her oversized mug.

The brat.

He leaned back in his chair, tilting back on two legs so Mia would think he was indifferent to her thinly veiled threat to auction him off to one of her bachelorette girlfriends.

"Yo, earth to Noah. Are you going to answer my question or not?"

"As a matter of fact, I have a date for your wedding."

"That was fast. Who is this amazing woman who's already worthy of an introduction to family?" Mia plunked her mug down, eyes wide.

He understood Mia's skepticism. His luck finding women was limited at best.

The last three women he dated seemed to want something from him, but none were willing to share what they wanted—like he was just supposed be this genius and figure it out.

At least Olivia had always told him exactly what she wanted, as well as when and how. There was never any guessing, and he liked the simplicity of not having to figure out whether no actually meant no or if she meant yes. In fact, it was the main reason he connected to her. Olivia had always said life was too short to not ask for what she wanted, and she'd been right.

When he decided to jump back into the marriage market,

he'd expected his next relationship to fall into place just as easily. Needless to say, the next few tries were disasters.

That's why Paige as his plus-one made perfect sense. She got him. They'd been friends forever. She knew and liked his family, laughed when they shared stories because she'd been part of some of them, and teased his siblings as mercilessly as they taunted her.

But most important, she was safe.

She knew how much he'd loved Olivia, and understood how difficult it was to move on. She wouldn't pressure him for more than he could give, and she'd keep his well-intentioned but meddling relatives from playing matchmaker.

"She's…someone I know you will like." He grinned, anticipating Mia's reaction when he finally revealed who he was bringing.

Memories of Paige's curly brown hair cascading down to the middle of her back made his fingers flex. When they were younger, he tried to grab one of her curls and stretch it out, only to watch it boing back into place. She pretended the action annoyed her, but it always made the specks of gold in her hazel eyes glint like treasure. He wondered if she still wore the out-of-control coils in a long ponytail like she did in high school.

Yes, Paige was the solution he needed. She was simple, uncomplicated, familiar. He was comfortable with her, and that somehow made reminiscing easier. Paige understood his pain. It was there, always. Without having to explain it or acknowledge it, they could share memories and focus on the joy instead of the sadness.

"Wait a minute." Mia's mouth dropped open, and her eyes narrowed in on him. "Are you telling me you're already serious about this woman?"

"No. She's a friend." The answer shot out of his mouth

before his brain caught up. "A good friend. Not someone I could ever have a relationship with."

"Bummer." Mia slouched in her seat. "For a minute there, I thought I was going to get my brother back."

He dropped his feet to the floor, the chair legs hitting the tile and jolting through his body. "What's that supposed to mean?"

"It means that since Olivia died, you haven't opened your heart to anyone, even family." Her eyebrows shot up while she called him out. "I don't care how many women you've dated. You always have an excuse for why none of them is relationship material."

"That's not true." The fib sounded weak, even to him.

"Please." Mia rolled her eyes. "Name one female you've loved since you left California."

He huffed out a breath and crossed his arms, desperate for a name. Then the idea struck. "Gracie," he tossed out.

His sister's silence thrilled him. Finally, he'd shut her up.

"Wasn't Gracie the Dachshund you had in Germany?"

Well, crap.

"You asked for the name of someone I loved, and I gave you a name."

"I asked you for the name of a woman, not a dog," Mia sputtered. "Bro, I'm worried about you."

"You shouldn't be. I'm fine. And you *are* going to like who I invited." He did his best to salvage the conversation before it got ugly and Mia started crying. He'd been warned many times about how sensitive brides could be, but never paid attention. Until now.

"Whose name should I put down? Spell it so the calligrapher gets it right."

"P-A-I-G-E." He popped each knuckle on his right hand.

"Paige? As in Paige Weaver?" Mia stared at him. Her eyes lit with surprise. "That's wonderful. I was worried she wouldn't come. I ran into her mom at the hospital in LA, believe it or not. She volunteers there. She's been begging Paige to come home for a visit, but, like you, she always has an excuse. I think there are too many painful memories here she hasn't come to terms with—like you." Mia took another sip of her coffee and settled back in her chair.

"In fact, I think spending time together will be beneficial for both of you. I still think it odd that you ended up with Olivia. My money was on Paige, and I lost the bet because of you."

"Me and Paige? Why would you bet on Paige?" Noah rested his forearms on the table and leaned closer to the computer camera lens to better gauge Mia's expression.

"Wow. Dude. You are so blind. You both loved video games, were into football, and never said no to going for long hikes, even when it was pouring rain or over a hundred degrees. Don't get me wrong, bro. We all loved Olivia, but I always thought you and Paige might…you know, end up together after Olivia died because…" Mia's words trailed off into a tense silence. "Never mind."

Mia's revelation sent shockwaves through his system. Him and Paige? The thought never occurred to him. She was a friend. Had been like a younger sister to him. She was always easy to hang out with. They liked the same types of food, had the same quirky sense of humor, and both loved to travel and immerse themselves into different cultures.

Besides Olivia, Paige was the most selfless, kindhearted person he knew. She was as dedicated to her students as she'd been to her sister.

And she'd been there for him when it counted.

No matter how many time zones separated them, she always picked up when he called. There had been a lot of lonely nights after Olivia died, and they spent hours on the phone chatting about music, movies—anything other than Olivia—to feel normal.

That was the sign of a true friend.

And he'd never ruin what they had by indulging in a casual relationship or muddying the waters with romance, no matter what Mia thought.

"Do me a favor, sis. Don't tell Mom, or anyone else for that matter. I want Paige's arrival to be a surprise." He yawned, the sunny yellow glow behind his sister emphasizing the time difference.

"Why don't you want anyone to know?" Mia frowned. "Everyone is going to be thrilled."

The question was a good one, but he didn't have a good answer. Mia's offhand comment about him and Paige had started his mind wondering about possibilities he'd never considered.

"Just keep this quiet. Don't make a big deal about it, or Mom will start dreaming about another wedding. I'll tell everyone when I get to California."

"Suit yourself." Mia wrote something on the sheet of paper and then finished her coffee. "I can't wait till you're home. It'll be the first time in years that all five of us Myers siblings are in the same place at the same time. Mom cries every time someone mentions it."

Warmth filled his heart at the thought of reuniting with his entire family: Mom, Julie, Kaylee, Logan, and Mia. His brothers-in-law, nieces, and nephews. He just wished his dad was still around to celebrate their reunion and have a beer on the back porch. Maybe his dad could have shed some light on his problem with women.

His sister certainly thought he had one.

Maybe that's why he got along with Paige so well. He didn't put her in the same category as all the others.

She was different.

Bold.

Adventurous.

Like the time she rode her bike twelve miles out to Old Man Wallace's lake, where he and his friends were skinny-dipping, hanging out, and having fun. They shouldn't have been swimming in the lake or loitering on private property, but summers in California were just too hot, and he and his buddies needed a distraction.

Apparently he was Paige's distraction. When she rolled up on her ten-speed, his friends scattered, racing for their shorts. She found their panic amusing, especially when she realized his shorts were out of reach and he was covering his private parts with a branch of poison ivy.

That day and the subsequent two weeks of painful rashes were forged in his memory. During his convalescence, Paige bought him a six-pack of sodas and a bag of Smarties as an apology, while still insisting she'd done nothing wrong. After all, he was the one trespassing.

Those were the good old days.

Startled to realize he was grinning, he sucked in a breath just as his computer dinged again.

His stomach dropped when he saw who the incoming call was from. *Mia and her big mouth.*

"Hello, Mother."

The damp gleam in her eyes confirmed his suspicion.

"Mia tells me you're bringing Paige to the wedding. Oh, Noah, I couldn't be more thrilled." She clutched her bathrobe and sniffled.

It was good his mother was thrilled now, because the minute he got stateside, the first thing he was going to do was pick Mia up and throw her in the nearest pool, clothes and all.

Chapter 3

wo weeks later

The Mineta San Jose International Airport buzzed with passengers racing to catch their flights, dragging their luggage behind them, or making a beeline toward the baggage claim area to pick up their bags and meet their loved ones. Paige wondered how many were reuniting with someone they'd secretly loved from afar.

Most moved past her with vigorous enthusiasm, a unique energy that was a combination of excitement, anticipation, and eager expectancy. It was easy to tell the vacationers from those who traveled for business by how they moved. The former scurried through the airport, fueled by a sense of adventure, while the latter slogged through the terminal, preoccupied with checking their phones for messages or exhausted by the routine travel that took them away from family and friends.

She wished she could feel something other than the melancholy that descended as soon as she started packing, although she hadn't been able to pinpoint the true source of her mood.

Part of her was excited to finally be home. To see familiar faces, eat at her favorite restaurants, visit her favorite parks, smell the ocean air. But then there was Noah. That was when the little black cloud of doubt appeared.

She rolled her shoulders and neck, trying to work out the aches from the fifteen-hour journey involving three connecting flights and reentry through Customs. She hitched the strap of her carry-on higher on her shoulder as she pulled her wheeled case behind.

She hoped Noah heeded her warning about bringing a car with enough trunk space for her five large suitcases, since she'd brought along everything she owned, minus the three huge boxes she shipped to her mom.

"Paige!"

The deep baritone shout made her stop and look around. She'd recognize Noah's voice anywhere. As the crowd parted like the fog lifting from a mountain valley, there he was.

Noah, she breathed, and took in his magnificence.

His long legs closed the distance between them quickly while she drank in the sight, all six feet of gorgeousness. God help her, the man had aged like fine wine. At forty, he was still the most attractive man she'd ever seen.

As a teenager, he was cute, with messy brown hair. As a man, his lean frame was now corded muscle. He'd tamed his hair with a neat, close-cropped style that flattered his strong jaw and high brow. And a few dashes of grey at his temples gave him a distinguished look that made more than a few women strolling through the airport take a second look.

Giddiness consumed her, and she remembered the day Kaylee, his second-oldest sister, declared Noah needed a haircut. She bullied and nagged until he agreed to sit on a stool in the kitchen for a trim. Noah had never worried much about his appearance, and she suspected Kaylee or one of his other sisters had already been after him to get a haircut for the wedding. She'd have to find out who to thank for the favor. No man looked more sexier or more fit in a pair of loose-fitting jeans and untucked shirt with his unruly curls falling over his forehead. She couldn't wait to see him in a suit for the wedding.

His dark eyes stared at her, pulling her in, and she had to remember to breathe. "Paige? Has it been so long you don't recognize me?"

She snapped out of her daze. *What is wrong with me?*

This was Noah, the guy she needed to hide her feelings from at all costs not simply because he'd forever be her sister's husband, but because there were consequences to him guessing her true motivation for traveling halfway across the globe to see him.

"Of course I recognize you." Her laugh sounded brittle. "It's just been so long. You've…changed."

"For the better, I hope." He looked her up and down while her body tingled in response. "You look exactly the same."

She supposed by "the same" he meant he still saw her as Olivia's kid sister. She swallowed her disappointment.

Closing his arms around her, he gave her a hug, making her body sigh. She'd forgotten the way his embrace made her troubles go away.

The last time he hugged her was sixteen years ago, and that hug was a different kind of hug. That hug occurred two days after Olivia's funeral and was meant to say goodbye— only Noah for some reason refused to let that be the end, which back then gave her hope. Now? Well, the hug was years ago, and not much had happened between them since. But, this hug was a definite hello.

"You're looking good." Paige nodded when he offered to take her roller bag. "It has been a long time."

"Thank you for coming." Noah glanced back at her since

he was doing his usual and was already half a step ahead. "I wasn't sure you would actually show."

He didn't know it, but three days ago, when she got an email from a friend begging her to take a school administrative job opening in Oman needing to be filled ASAP, she almost backed out of the trip. She'd always wanted to visit the eastern side of the Arabian Peninsula. The salary was almost double what she'd been earning in Vietnam, and she'd heard good things about living in the United Arab Emirates. The offer was tempting, but she'd promised Noah.

More important, she'd promised herself. A vow to confront the painful memories keeping her away from home for so many years. Even if she decided not to stay in the US, she was tired of running from the past, and needed to face and finish with the hurt she'd been avoiding.

Noah grabbed the railing of the escalator down to the baggage claim area. "How was your flight?"

"Long." She rolled her shoulders, feeling every knot.

"Hungry?"

"Nope. I ate on the plane. Thanks for asking."

She wondered when this small talk would end.

Strange she sensed an awkwardness with him, because he'd never shown the slightest bit of uneasiness around her before. She set her mind to finding something to ease the tension. "So, tell me the truth. Has Mia turned into Bridezilla yet?"

A deep, rich chuckle spilled out of him, and she reveled in the sensations conjured by his crooked smile. "She's getting close."

Ah, there they were, those deep dimples she missed, one on each side of his sensual mouth.

Noah skirted around the baggage carousel as the belt began to turn and luggage rolled up from somewhere below. She pointed out her bags and enjoyed the view as he leaned over to retrieve the first black bag. She kept pointing until Noah had stacked them all onto a cart.

The growing mountain of luggage drew other travelers' attention, and she shrugged off the curious stares with a friendly tilt of her mouth. As an experienced world traveler, she was accustomed to inquisitiveness.

When all the bags were accounted for, Noah led the way to the parking garage. Taking his usual long strides, he led her out of the busy airport while she double-timed it just to keep up. Exactly like the good old days.

Noah held out a key fob, and the lights of a huge black truck, undoubtedly built for more rugged terrain, not California highways, flashed. The massive truck had enormous tires and a hitch that could pull an oversized horse trailer.

"Is this Brent's truck?" she asked. "I can't imagine it's a rental."

"Yep."

Julie, Noah's oldest sister, and her husband, Brent, had a spread up north, and since Julie had always been an animal lover, they probably had horses, cows, sheep, and chickens, and all excellent reasons to have a big truck.

"I'm surprised Brent let you borrow his truck."

Noah gave her a mischievous grin. "He didn't." He shrugged. "I was going to drive my rental, but I couldn't find the keys and didn't want to be late. Julie told me if I so much as scratch this thing, Brent will have me unloading hay for a month."

"Sounds like Julie." Paige pictured the tall, lean woman, who reminded her of a riding crop in both stature and personality—strong, sturdy, always one to guide her children and animals in the right direction. She'd always liked Noah's eldest sister, even though she was ten years older. Julie's personality was as big as California, and she always treated Paige with patience and kindness.

Noah closed the tailgate, patting the vehicle. "Nice boy." He laughed at his own inside joke.

Noah's playful side had always made her heart pit-a-pat a little bit harder. In some ways Noah would never grow old.

"Thanks for picking me up." Paige climbed into the passenger seat and locked her seatbelt. The size of the vehicle, such a contrast to the tiny cars and scooters common overseas, made it very clear she was home.

He put the key in the ignition and shrugged off her gratitude. "You're my plus-one."

The coil of uneasiness bothering her for the past two weeks cinched tighter. She wasn't sure how she felt about being Noah's *plus-one*. She'd fantasized for years about going on a real date with him, but this wasn't a date. They were simply attending Mia's wedding together, which meant neither of them had to find someone to sit next to or dance with—a bonus in some ways.

"Tell me about Vietnam. Seems like an interesting place." Noah pulled his credit card out of the parking ticket machine and rolled toward the highway exit.

"Have you ever been there?" Paige asked while admiring how the car behind them slowed down enough to let them merge into the flow of vehicles. She'd forgotten how civilized traffic could be. In Vietnam, it tended to be a free-for-all, with cars, scooters, and buses all vying for the same space at the same time.

"Not yet. It's on my list." Noah glanced at her. "I kept thinking I'd get over there to see you since Singapore is so close, but…well, something always came up."

That something was Olivia. The common thread that drew the three of them together. And once the thread was broken, they were forced forever apart.

They were both running from their demons. Like her, he seemed to find a job in another country every two years —a nice way of hiding from friends and family.

"How was your spring semester?" His quick glance at her and then back to the road revealed genuine interest. "Did you have any star students?"

"Every semester, every class, every student is different. There was one young man, Hoang Uyen. He always arrived early for class and insisted on sitting in the very first row." The warmth of the memory cascaded though her as she remembered his silly grin. "The first day he walked in with his shoulders back, chin high, and announced to everyone that he wanted to learn English to impress his grandmother. After a bit of teasing from the other students, he took his seat. Later I found out he was teaching his mother English at night. They were both so eager to learn."

She took a deep breath and felt the tension ease out of her shoulders. "On my days off I meet—met—Nguyen, Hoang's mother, at a small coffee shop not too far from her home. She's a dedicated student, and we have become friends."

She wondered what Hoang would think of California. She glanced over her shoulder as Noah changed lanes. The traffic had lightened, and she was glad they had turned north and were out of the heavier city traffic.

"What about you?" Paige settled back into her seat. "Working on any new projects?"

"I have a couple." Noah drove with one hand on the top of the steering wheel, the other tapping his leg in time with the country tune on the radio.

His movements seemed less stiff, but there was still something agitating him. When he was irritated he tended to grind his teeth and his jaw muscles were keeping time with his fingers. Was it her? Was he worried about his job? Was there some complication with the wedding? Or was it something else? Was he dealing with ghosts and regrets about Olivia? She shifted in her seat, unable to get comfortable, and, as they rolled into town, decided to give it time as her past once again became her present.

"I'm doing a new website design for the resort where we're staying. I can't wait for you to see the place. It's gorgeous, and well worth every minute in an uncomfortable airplane seat. There's a vineyard, stables, and a great pool. And the people who own it, the Fosters, are talented, organized, grounded, and very likeable."

"I looked it up online before I left," Paige rotated a bit toward Noah. "I discovered Nate Keller and his son won a World Chef competition not too long ago. I bet the food's amazing."

"Nate's a really nice guy." He flicked on the turn signal and moved into another lane to pass a slow-moving sedan. "Connor is going to give his dad a run for the money. He made this beef Wellington the other night that was outstanding. The best I've ever eaten—it was memorable."

"I can't wait for the wedding reception, then." She studied Noah's handsome profile. "The wedding invitation indicated cocktail attire. I emailed Mia with a picture of the dress I bought to see if it was appropriate, but I didn't hear back from her. It's been ages since I've attended a formal event in the US, and customs can be very different in other countries."

"You? In a dress? This I have to see."

She chuckled over his exaggerated surprise. She'd come a long way from the tomboyish girl he used to know.

Growing up, she preferred to climb a tree, go fishing, or play with her golden retriever, rather than play tea party, dress-up, or dolls. Those were Olivia's thing. Paige's choice of activities could be summed up as rough and tumble compared to Olivia's perfume and lace.

Her sister aspired to be on the cover of *Teen USA,* whereas Paige preferred to be front and center in her soccer team's photograph.

Back then Paige couldn't be bothered with makeup and fashion. There were too many things to discover, too many exciting challenges to be tackled. Wherever there was an adventure, Paige could be found in her jeans, sneakers, and T-shirts, with her long, curly hair in a simple ponytail or messy braid.

"I still can't believe you settled into teaching. I always thought you'd be a race car driver or investigative journalist or some type of sports superstar. A teacher just seems..." His expression turned thoughtful, and she suspected he was trying to think of the appropriate word.

"Common?" she suggested.

"I was going to say structured."

"What a nice way to say boring," she crossed her arms, but wasn't sure why she felt a little defensive.

She used to believe the same thing about working inside all day. Teaching kids to speak English sounded like a dull grind. She'd never been a great student, too distracted and anxious to move on to something active and exciting rather than focus on homework and lessons. When she told her sixth grade science teacher about her dream of becoming an astronaut, Mr. King then explained the importance of good grades and how she'd have to study if she wanted to be given such a lofty opportunity.

By the time she was eighteen, every long-term dream she had was squashed. If Olivia's death taught her anything, it was that life is short and unfair. Right then and there she decided there was no way she was going to spend her limited time on earth with her nose in a book.

She wanted to see the world.

"I never would have predicted you'd be a digital nomad,

Mr. Technology. I always pictured you and Oli—" Heat rolled into her chest as she pummeled herself for going there.

A strained silence saturated the truck's cab. She looked away, pretending fascination with the landscape flying by.

He cleared his throat. "I took some online computer design courses so I could work from home."

Left unsaid was that working from home enabled him to take care of Olivia while the cancer slowly and inexorably stole her life. "What I learned allows me to live anywhere I want. It's not a bad life if you can keep the jobs coming in. Problem is, I spend half my time doing work, and the other half searching for work.".

Boy, aren't we a pair? A pair of misfits.

She relaxed against the leather seat back, feeling the drain of the past twenty-four hours of travel. Her mind drifted, and her eyelids grew heavy. She tried focusing on the passing scenery, but the lull of the tires' hum against the pavement was too hypnotic.

When the truck's engine changed to a growl, she jerked awake. "Oh, sorry. I must have fallen asleep." She looked around and discovered they'd turned off the highway onto a two-lane blacktop road.

"Jet lag. I get it." Noah glanced from her to the road several times and nibbled on the side of his lip.

"Whatever it is, ask your question." Clearly he'd been thinking while she napped, and she wasn't sure whether that was a good thing.

"I'm curious. Why did you go into teaching?"

Of all the questions he could have asked, she wasn't expecting such an easy one.

"Teaching wasn't something I planned. I just fell into it. I was waitressing in Prague and met Diamond. She's British and a bit bossy. She told me that instead of wasting my life waitressing around Europe, I should get a TEFL certificate.

The pay was good, and I could load up my bank account. With a TEFL certificate, I could get a job most anywhere. Standing on my feet all day and smelling like restaurant food 24/7 was getting old, so I applied to an online school and started studying at night."

"She actually said you were wasting your life?"

"She did." Paige rubbed the sleep from her eyes and sat up straighter. "I hope you get to meet her one day. She's this tiny woman, barely five feet tall. She now has four kids and a husband who adores her. When I met her, she'd just taken a leave of absence from nursing school and found herself in Prague, waiting tables with the likes of me. At the time Diamond had been trying to find her place in the world."

"I bet you're the cool teacher and the kids love you." Noah grinned, but her gut told her something wasn't right.

She studied his face. "Why don't you ask me the question you're really wondering about? The one about Olivia?"

His hands tightened around the steering wheel, his knuckles white. "You just got here, and I figure you must be exhausted from travel. There will be time for all that later."

By *all that*, she assumed he meant the emotional baggage neither of them had fully dealt with. The subject both of them had avoided for years. The one she still wanted to avoid.

She stretched out her legs. "What's on the agenda for the next few days besides a wedding?"

She shifted closer to listen to the half dozen things he rattled off. He talked about Alec, the guy Mia was marrying, and his newest nephew, the youngest of Kaylee's five. He gave her some insight into his older brother's plan to start a digital marketing company and confessed Logan was trying to get Noah to work for him. Which was smart on Logan's part, because Noah was a computer genius.

"Have you played any good video games lately?" She smoothed back a wayward curl tickling her neck.

His eyes brightened. "Oh, man. Did you see The Keystone Prophecy just released their latest version? It is so GOAT." He pounded the steering wheel enthusiastically.

"Goat? Like in smelly farm animals?"

"You *have* been gone a long time." His face turned red as she chuckled, and he looked at her. "GOAT, as in greatest of all time."

"Ohh." She drew out the word as comprehension dawned. "That term hasn't made it into the Vietnamese dictionary yet." With an assessing, sidelong glance, Paige wondered what other terms she'd add to her collection this weekend while she and Noah got reacquainted.

Chapter 4

$\mathcal{N}$oah's phone vibrated in the dash holder, and he glanced at the display to see his second oldest sister, Kaylee, was calling. He hit the green button to accept the video call. An image of a freckle-faced girl with a missing front tooth appeared on the screen.

"Hi, Uncle Noah!"

"Riley?" Noah took a quick glance at the screen. "Does your mom know you're calling me?"

"No." The little girl covered her mouth with her hand to muffle her giggle. "When're you coming back? You said we'd do something together today."

"We're almost there," he said with more patience than he felt. "Hurry and give the phone back to your mom, or you might find yourself in a time-out when the fun starts."

"Is your girlfriend with you?" Riley's innocent question made it clear the rest of the family had been talking about him and Paige. "Is she pretty?"

His eyes automatically slanted right for a look, and he shivered as raw, sexual awareness gut-punched him. Paige was more than pretty. As a kid and young teen she had a wholesome kind of appeal, but as a mature woman, her independence and world experiences had added layers of complexity to her allure.

Her hair, a lustrous brown, was streaked with red and gold highlights from hours in the sun. Even in jeans and a light sweater, it was obvious her body was toned. Her face was sun-kissed and a few faint lines at the corners of her eyes testified she smiled and laughed often.

The jittery energy radiating off her when she was young was still there, but it seemed she'd learned to harness and conserve it. He had no doubt once she was swimming or hiking or horseback riding, her unleashed, vibrant spirit would appear.

"You can tell me what you think when you meet her." His voice softened. It was impossible to stay strict with any of his nieces or nephews, a fact they quickly discovered. He had to admit, Uncle Noah was a pushover, and they took advantage of his lack of parental experience every chance they got. "Give the phone back to your mom, and we'll see you in a few."

He caught Paige's curious look.

"That was Riley, Kaylee's oldest daughter. She's eight going on eighteen, and she loves stealing my sister's phone. The little snot calls the family one at a time until someone answers. She has no concept of time zones, so I usually get calls at two in the morning."

"I've seen pictures of Kaylee's kids on her Instagram page." Paige chuckled. "Riley looks spunky like her mom. Is the whole family going to be at the wedding?"

A nervous tension crept up his back and pinched his shoulders. "Yep. Everyone. Even the ones I haven't seen in years." And some who weren't expected.

Paige squinted while she scanned his face. Her scrutiny provoked a tickle in the back of his throat.

He coughed and looked out the window to avoid her stare. "Look at those clouds. It's going to be a pretty sunset tonight."

"Noah? What are you hiding?"

"Me? Hiding something? Why would you ask that?"

Paige crossed her arms.

Oh, man. He gulped. "Well, it's just that… Did I tell you my Aunt Rosa decided to come to the wedding at the last minute?"

"If I remember right, she's the one who likes to play poker, smoke cigars, and drink whisky?"

"Bourbon, but yeah, that's her. She and my cousins decided to attend at the last minute and are driving up from San Diego."

"And you're telling me this, why?" Paige's glare now had annoyance added in.

"Well, you see…um…"

"Let me guess. Your nice two-bedroom cottage on the ocean has been reassigned to your aunt and cousins. Am I right?"

He scratched an itch on his neck not there. "Well, you see—"

"Am I right?"

He took a peek to check how annoyed she was, because if she'd dumped him in the same situation, he'd be fighting mad. He let out a long sigh. "Yep. You guessed right."

"Thought so. Where are we staying instead?" she asked as they wound their way up the curved drive to the Silver Fox Resort. He pointed to the ridge looking out over the ocean. "We're staying in one of the larger villas…with the rest of the family."

"When were you going to tell me about the change?"

"You were always the go-with-the-flow type, so I thought I'd surprise you."

She crossed her arms. "Un-huh. You are such a guy. And a bad liar too."

"Don't be mad. Please. Mom promised we could have the cottage down by the ocean all to ourselves after the wedding, when Aunt Rosa leaves." That suggested a degree of intimacy he had not meant to imply. "I mean, not that we need privacy, to do, you know, ah…I reserved the private cottage so I could work on the resort's new website without a hundred distractions. And Mom wants to make sure you have some peace and quiet to relax. After all, I promised you a vacation."

"Stop, before you dig an even deeper hole." Paige grinned and shook her head. "Your mom is sweet, but is always matchmaking. I'm afraid she will be disappointed this time."

"She's really looking forward to seeing you." His shoulders sagged with relief because she wasn't angry about the change in accommodations. "Thanks for being flexible about this."

"It doesn't matter where I sleep." She chuckled and shook her head. "I didn't pay for this trip anyway. You did. Just promise me a hot shower and a place where I can curl up to sleep undisturbed for the next few hours and I'll be fine."

Noah remembered the running feet and giddy screaming at five a.m. that morning and cringed. When he got up at six, there was already a lineup at the bathroom door.

"I'll make sure you get a shower and some sleep." He turned into the villa parking lot, looking for an empty spot amid the swarm of vehicles.

"How many people did you say were going to be here?"

He hadn't. On purpose.

He managed to find a space and pulled in. "When I said everyone is here, I literally meant everyone."

"Oh." Her voice was faint and a little panicked. "It's been a long time since I've been home, around so many people from…well…before."

"I know. It's been a bit overwhelming for me as well."

She leaned and dropped her forehead in her hands, her elbows balancing on her knees. He quickly unlatched his seatbelt and rested his hand on her back while guilt tightened his gut like a vise closing around two pieces of wood and soured the taste in his mouth.

"Paige. What can I say to make it better?"

She sat up, her face red with suppressed laughter. "You have to admit, this is way too funny. Your mom never could say no. I bet she's in there right now, cooking for thirty people."

He glanced at the villa. "The last count I heard was twenty-two."

Paige threw her head back, and he couldn't remember the last time he'd seen something so beautiful.

She pushed her thick curls over her shoulder as her desperate attempts to stop laughing failed.

"I'm glad you're laughing now, because I'm afraid you won't be laughing tomorrow morning when my nieces and nephews are up before the sun."

"One good thing about jet lag, I'll already be awake."

Right there was the reason he always made sure to keep in touch with Paige. She was a breath of fresh air compared to his temperamental sisters. *Life was too short to sweat the small stuff,* popped out of his memory box of sayings.

And she was right. For some, life was way, way too short.

He startled at a knock on the truck window.

When he turned, he was greeted by his mom and Mia's happy faces.

He opened the door slowly, allowing them time to move back.

"We couldn't wait. We're so excited, we couldn't wait to say hi to Paige." His mother shuffled around the hood of the truck. "Paige. I'm so glad you're here. Noah said you might be staying awhile."

Paige's eyes flared and sought his as his mother pulled her in for a big-bosomed hug. He ducked behind the cab and moved to get her luggage.

"You're a jerk." Mia appeared beside him and grabbed for the next suitcase on the stack "I can tell by that look—you didn't tell her."

"Tell who what?" He hauled out one of the big suitcases.

Mia punched in him the arm.

"Ow. What was that for?" He set the bag on the ground and rubbed his shoulder.

"You didn't tell Paige about the room change or this mess. I bet you told her it was going to be a nice family gathering, where she could rest and relax and enjoy her time at the beach."

He moved an arm's length away from Mia and reached for another suitcase. "You know how laid-back Paige is."

"I do, but that doesn't give you an out." Mia reached for one of the bags to extend the roller handle. "You don't like confrontations. Never have. But while she's here, you need to clear the air."

He glared at Mia. "Stay out of this."

Mia stepped into his space, her head barely reaching his chin. "If you both keep refusing to lay the past to rest, I'm going to lock you in a room together until you sort things out. I love you both, and I want the best for both of you. If it isn't now, then when?"

This was why he didn't like living near family. He'd changed continents to avoid moments like this.

"I get it, Mia. Now, will you get off my toes?"

Mia stepped back and studied his face. Satisfied for now, she moved the roller case aside, grabbed the smallest of the suitcases, and headed for the villa.

He rubbed his jaw.

The temptation to get in the truck and head on up to Brent and Julie's ranch struck hard, but he would never leave Paige behind to fend for herself.

If anyone in the world deserved to be happy, it was Paige. Leaving her to deal with his meddling family was a sure way to guarantee her unhappiness. He squared his shoulders and entered the family fray.

Chapter 5

*P*aige walked beside Mrs. Myers while she chatted away, letting Paige know dinner would be available soon and clean towels had been set aside. The older woman's brown hair had turned gray, but the family matriarch's smile was just as swift as her reprimands when a rule was broken. At the core, she had a good heart, one that never degraded anyone's soul.

"It's been too long. Noah and Mia give me updates from time to time, but it's not the same as seeing you. I've missed our chats."

"I brought you some of my favorite coffee from Vietnam." Paige felt herself easing into the familiarity of home, thanks to Mrs. Myers' gentle, take-charge manner.

The salty ocean air and pine-scented breeze were just like she remembered, but the impact of the resort's stunning coastal vista made her chest tight with regret for not returning sooner. The wooded cliffs and rocky shore had been her playground growing up, and in some ways it made her feel like she was sixteen again.

She slowed and deepened her breathing to keep her

emotions in check. "If there is a day that's quiet, maybe we can sneak away for some coffee and a catch-up."

"I'd like that, dear." Mrs. Myers stopped in the middle of the walkway and slipped her arm across Paige's shoulders. "Thank you for coming. I know this gathering will do you and Noah a world of good. You need to be around family."

"Mom, you promised," Noah said, coming up the sidewalk loaded down with Paige's luggage.

"Here, let me help." She reached for the leather bag Noah had across his shoulder.

"I got it. You go on ahead, since everyone's waiting for you."

Mrs. Myers moved her arm to circle around Paige's waist to guide her inside. "How was your journey, dear?"

"Long, but I made all my connections and my luggage arrived at the same time I did, so I can't complain." She stepped into a spacious villa decorated with warm colors. The floor looked like aged wood, but when she stepped on the surface, the brown and gray six-inch tiles had a porcelain feel. The warm gray walls were welcoming, as were the large sectional couch and stone fireplace.

A group of youngsters sat on the floor playing a board game, and the aroma coming from the kitchen was a heavenly blend of garlic and onion. Pasta night, she guessed.

Noah's two oldest sisters had command of the kitchen, with knives out, busy chopping up lettuce and tomatoes.

"Don't mind the mess," Mrs. Myers said. "We put you in the third bedroom with Noah."

An explosion of terror made her legs stop working. "Uh, Mrs. Myers. Um, I don't think—"

"Oh, don't worry. It's okay. No one minds if you sleep together. You're both adults." Mrs. Myers continued on, oblivious of Paige stumbling down the hall after her. "It was at a family wedding such as this when my cousin found love in the arms of the groom's best man, and they've been happily married for thirty years."

I'm going to strangle Noah, she thought.

"Mrs. Myers…" she began, ready to set the record straight.

The mother of five opened the door and grinned sheepishly.

Paige let out a relieved sigh.

Wooden-slat bunk beds with a ladder were pushed up against the far well. Mrs. Myers always had a dry sense of humor, and this had to be another one of her stunts.

"I guess Noah and I will have to decide who gets to be on top." Paige winked, playing along now she had an idea of what was going on.

"That, young lady, is one of the best comebacks I've heard in a long time. I knew you had spunk." Mrs. Myers patted her cheek. "Take a nap, dear. Dinner will be available for you whenever you wake." She searched Paige's face. "I hope you know you are family. Always will be. Can't ever get rid of us now." Mrs. Myers turned and shuffled off down the hall, herding the grandchildren who'd gathered to see what the fuss was all about back into the living room.

Next came Noah, pulling her suitcases behind him. "Go ahead. Yell at me now. Get it over with."

"Is this the last of the surprises, or are there more?" Paige set her bag down on the bottom bunk, because more than anything she couldn't wait to watch Noah crawl his way into the upper bunk. Every night.

"Enough surprises for one day, don't you think?" he asked, his eyes softening. "Thanks for understanding."

"That's what friends are for."

His gaze held hers for a long moment. "You've always been more than a friend."

Oh, here it comes.

"Yes, a little sister." She tried to laugh it off, but the image she knew he had of her always hurt, especially because at one point he was her everything. She turned away, pretending to find something in her carry-on. What she needed was a tissue, because as jet lagged as she was, she just might cry.

"That wasn't what I was going to say."

She froze, and then straightened to peek over her shoulder. "What were you going to say?"

He shoved his hands in his pockets, and for a minute she thought he'd changed his mind, because he glanced around the room—everywhere but at her.

"I don't know how to describe it. You've always been like my anchor. Wherever I was in the world, I knew you were out there as well. Just knowing gave me comfort." He grew quiet and then pointed at her suitcases. "I'll leave you to get settled."

He left before she could think of anything to say.

She sank down on the bed, not sure what to make of what he said. For the first time in her life, she had proof Noah viewed her in a context outside the role of Olivia's little sister.

He saw her. Actually saw *her*.

She trembled at the implication. Did that mean Noah might see her as a woman? Someone to love?

And, even if by some miracle he did, was his love for her bigger than the memory of Olivia, an embellished love blown way out of proportion over the years?

Chapter 6

*N*oah stuck out his tongue and jiggled Max, his three-month-old nephew, to make the baby laugh.

Kaylee's Max was a surprise to the family, since Kaylee and John had been convinced they were done having kids. Max was a contented little guy, most likely because Kaylee was so laid-back with her fifth child. Noah hadn't been around much when the other four were born, so he'd informed everyone upon arriving he was going to spend quality time with all his nieces and nephews to make up for the missed opportunities.

"I should get him changed." Kaylee carried empty bowls of what had been ice cream dessert and stacked them on the counter.

"Already done." He blew a raspberry against Max's belly.

Kaylee stopped in mid-dishwasher load. "You changed Max? Did you use ointment?"

"Just like you showed me. I'm not six anymore."

She closed her eyes. "No. Of course not. I'm sorry, Noah."

"For?" He lifted Max higher in the air.

"You're my baby brother. Sometimes it's hard to remember you're forty." Her eyes got huge. "Wow. Forty. My baby brother is old."

"If I'm old, what does that make you?"

"Ancient." His sister laughed. "Life sure hasn't turned out like I thought it would."

Curious, he got to his feet and swayed his way across the kitchen while Max's eyes grew heavy. "What did you expect?"

"We were all so close, I thought we'd buy houses ten minutes apart and get together every Sunday for big family dinners. Instead, you're globe-trotting, Mia and Alec are in Los Angeles, and Julie and Brent are up north."

"Logan's around."

"Yeah, he's around to help Mom, but we hardly ever see him. It's hard when our schedules are so packed, and we're taking kids to lessons or soccer games every other day."

"We've all learned life doesn't go according to plan." He looked at Max, trying to envision what his and Olivia's children might have looked like. "Even if we don't live ten minutes from one another, we're still close. Nothing will change. And it just makes gatherings like this all the more important."

Kaylee lifted onto her tiptoes and kissed his cheek. "I know."

A soft feminine harrumph interrupted the moment.

"I don't mean to intrude." A rumpled Paige pointed over her shoulder toward the bedroom, her hair mussed, cheeks still pink from sleeping. "I'll come back later."

"Don't be ridiculous. Noah and I were having a philosophical discussion and getting way too deep," Kaylee replied. "I hope you're hungry. We fixed you a plate. There's salad, bread, and penne Bolognese with your name on it."

Kaylee pulled covered containers out of the refrigerator that indeed had Paige's name written on them in a child's scrawl on a bright yellow post-it note stuck to the lid. "Riley, my oldest, helped with the labels. She made sure we saved you some chocolate cake, too."

"Sounds perfect." Paige gently patted the baby's diaper-covered rump. "Who's this little guy?"

"This is Max." Noah tilted the baby up so she could see him. "He'll be three months old tomorrow."

Both women looked impressed because he knew.

"What? I'm just trying to be a good uncle."

"You are doing a mighty fine job, Uncle Noah." Kaylee set the leftovers in the microwave and pressed the start button.

Paige accepted the salad and fork Kaylee handed her. "The house is quiet. Where is everyone?"

"Shh," Noah chided. "Don't say that too loud or you'll jinx everything. They're on a snipe hunt along the beginner hiking trail. Mom got flashlights for everyone from Amy Denham, the resort's concierge, and promised the first one to find a snipe egg could pick which movie to watch when they get back. I think it was her way of keeping everyone quiet so you could sleep."

Was that a blush turning Paige's cheeks red? He liked the look. It suited her. Then again, he liked a lot of what he saw. She'd put her hair up, so only a few curly tendrils hung down, and she'd washed her face, which glowed with a renewed freshness. The natural look suited her. She couldn't have been more gorgeous.

"Snipe hunt, huh?" Paige sat on a stool on the far side of the kitchen counter. "You and Olivia took me and Mia on a snipe hunt once. We were so mad when we learned there is no such animal."

They exchanged an intimate look about the shared memory.

"We made it up to you and Mia," Noah pointed out. "Didn't we take you bowling? Or was it roller-skating?"

"Sorry to interrupt the walk down memory lane, but let Paige eat first." Kaylee set the pasta in front of her. "Your slice of cake is over there on the counter." She pointed to the plastic tub with a blue lid.

"There is?" Noah lifted the lid to take a sniff.

"I wasn't offering the cake to you, Flake. You already had more than your share." Kaylee wagged a finger at him. He wanted to waggle a finger back for calling him by his nickname of old.

"Did not." Noah said. "Your oldest two took off with half my portion."

"And you let them," Kaylee reminded him.

Noah handed Max to Kaylee. "Fine. I'll be a gentleman and leave the rest for Paige."

Paige looked up from pouring dressing on her salad. "I hate seeing a grown man pout. If you want, I'll share."

He pointed at Paige and took a seat next to her. "Now that, right there, is one reason why I like you."

"Oh, Lord. It's getting rather too sweet in here for my taste. I'll let you two catch up." Kaylee grabbed a pacifier off the counter and headed toward the living room area.

Paige forked pasta into her mouth. "This is really good. I'm in carb heaven."

"I bet you don't find delicious pasta in Vietnam."

"Pasta? No. The cuisine is great, just different. When I'm cooking, my favorite meal is roasted octopus."

"I'm still getting used to the exotic cuisine in other countries." He pounded his chest and made a choking sound. "Roasted beetles. Buffalo penis soup. Raw sago worms. Give me a burger any day, and I'm happy."

"Octopus tastes way better than a burger. You should try it." She was serious.

"I'll pass, thanks."

"Says the boy who ate spiders." Paige gave him a sideways glance.

He groaned. "That was a dare, and I can't believe you remember that."

"You loved the attention." Paige picked through her salad, moving mushrooms to the side, then loaded her fork and gave him an expectant look.

"Maybe a little," he admitted.

He'd been at a neighborhood birthday party when some kids came up with the dare. Whoever ate the most spiders won a prize. He couldn't remember what the prize was, but he'd been called Spider Boy for the rest of the school year. Someone even drew a cartoon picture with a picture of his face inserted into the drawing.

"I'm Spider Boy." He wiggled his eyebrows. "Everyone loves a superhero."

Paige covered her mouth and laughed. "Superhero?"

He flexed his bicep. "I even had my mom make me a cape."

"The title fits."

Her eyes turned sad, and he hated that he'd landed upon a memory which erased the joy from her expression.

"Hey. I forgot." She pulled her phone out of her back pocket, opened the gallery app, and handed him the device. "I took pictures of some of my students. I thought you might like to see. Just swipe."

The joy he wished he hadn't just ruined for her filled him. He swiped through the pictures of kids who looked to be between ten and sixteen. Each picture was different, but each student had a look of adoration in their eyes as they gazed at her. He understood that feeling all too well.

"That's Hoang, the boy I told you about. And that's Hai. She's only twelve, but is one of the smartest kids ever. She has an IQ of 140."

Noah whistled and gave her a disbelieving look. "This little girl?"

Paige nodded. "Yes, that little girl, and she's so shy and sweet. There's the little boy she has a crush on. They sit together every day at lunch, and she shares her orange with him. After class she stays behind to make sure the books are in order and put away properly.

"That's Ricky," she grabbed his hand and turned the screen her way. "He's in a pop band, and fancies himself westernized. The truth is, I don't think he knows what westernized means. The only reason he takes English is because he dreams of getting a US music contract."

The heat from her touch had melted a few brain cells, and he had to work to remember where they were in the conversation. "Will you get the same kids in your class next year?" He rested the phone on the counter near Paige's napkin.

She stopped eating and started pushing the pasta around her bowl.

"Paige? What is it?"

"No, I won't have the same kids next year." Her eyes were sad.

Was she on the verge of tears?

"I'm not going back to Vietnam after the wedding is over. I didn't renew the contract. It's a good time for a change. I'm not sure what I'm going to do next, but I need something new. Different. There was a job offer, but I turned it down to come here."

"What?" He sat up straighter.

"It's time for me to move on." She pushed the bowl away. "There's more competition for teaching jobs, and, as much as I enjoyed living in Vietnam, it seems I can't make myself stay anywhere longer than one or two years. "There are too many things to see and do. Olivia thought she had all the time in the world, especially after she beat the cancer once. Every year she was healthy, our worries about the cancer returning lessened. But now I feel like I need to do everything on my bucket list, just in case."

By which she meant, just in case cancer came along. The Big C ran in her family genes. The odds of her getting sick were higher than her getting hit by a car.

He didn't have a family history of cancer, but he'd been infected with the fear as well, and had a similar sense of urgency to be and do everything now.

Paige, it seemed, was still confronting her fear.

"Wow. This is big news." Noah leaned in. "What about your apartment? All your stuff?"

"Didn't you wonder why I had five suitcases? What you lugged in is everything I own, minus several boxes I shipped to my mom. She said I could stay with her until I decide what's next. I'm headed down to LA after the wedding." She stopped, took a deep breath, then met his eyes. "I'm thinking it might be time to come home. For good."

That wouldn't be an easy decision, Noah realized, as soon as he applied it to himself. He wondered if Paige was prepared to confront her past in order to look ahead to the future.

His mom and siblings had been hinting it would be nice to again have him back in Oakland. He was surprised at how easy it had been to transition into the California lifestyle for the few days he'd been back so far, but staying was way different than visiting.

"How do you feel about moving back?"

"A little scared," she admitted. "Excited. Relieved. Indecisive. Maybe that's why I let you talk me into attending the wedding. Deep down, I wanted to be convinced to come home. Now I'm here…" She shrugged.

He'd considered the idea of returning to California, being

closer to family, but hadn't been as bold. Coming home was a reminder of what he was missing, but he wasn't yet ready to make a decision the way Paige had.

Her courage was inspiring.

What if he made a similar move?

What if he settled in California…close to Paige?

It would be easier to fight the demons still lurking around the two of them if they could do it together.

The idea was so compelling he almost said something, but then clenched his jaw. Now wasn't the time, but it definitely gave him something to think about.

Chapter 7

*E*arly the following afternoon, Paige sat in the corner of the couch sectional with her computer in her lap, trying to clear her emails from the past couple of days. A friend had emailed about a teaching job in Japan, but accepting it would have felt like moving backwards. Until she made a decision about where she wanted to settle, she couldn't even begin thinking about a job.

She was in the process of blowing out a frustrated breath when a pair of wide blue eyes peered over her computer screen, followed by a giggle.

Paige closed her laptop to reveal Kaylee's six-year-old, hunkered down on the floor at her feet.

"Whatcha got there?" Paige pointed at the stuffed white unicorn in Emma's arms.

"Pokey." Emma's nose scrunched as she giggled and stood up to show off the stuffed toy.

"You're Emma. Do I have that right?"

The little princess with pigtails and bright blue eyes nodded.

"Why don't you come up here and sit next to me, and we

can make up a story." Paige set her computer aside and patted the couch next to her.

Emma crawled up, sat on the couch, and then scootched back until she was against the cushion, her big eyes expectant.

"Pokey, huh?" Paige placed an arm around Emma, pulling her closer to her side, and pointed to the once-white bundle of fabric with bare spots and now brown with age. "Once upon a time, there was a unicorn named Pokey, and he was very proud of his horn's colors of pink, purple, and teal." She touched the sparkly plush fabric. "One day, while hanging out in the forest, he saw an old man limping along the road, carrying a bundle of hay. Do you know what the unicorn did?"

"No. What?" Emma's eyes rounded as she looked at the stuffed unicorn.

"Pokey said, 'May I carry your bundle of hay?' because that's what good unicorns do. They help others. The old man gave the hay to the unicorn so Pokey could carry the bundle to his home. The unicorn, seeing the man needed even more help, stayed to plow his fields and carry firewood. He worked day after day, and the man gave him not one word of thanks. Do you know what the unicorn did then?"

"Tell me," Emma pleaded.

"The unicorn went away, and do you know why?"

Emma shook her head.

"Because," Paige drew out the word, "because even unicorns need to be told they are loved and appreciated. So, remember—if someone does something nice for you, you should thank them. It will make them feel special."

Emma pulled on one of her ponytails, the story meaning sinking in. "Oh, I get it." Her eyes brightened. "Thank you, Aunt Paige. I like your story." Emma leaned up to kiss her cheek and then rolled off the couch.

Aunt Paige? Paige set her fingertips where Emma's warm lips had been. Well, technically, she was something akin to an aunt.

"Aunt Paige, do you have a minute?" Charlotte, or Charley, as most of the family referred to her, was Julie and Brent's daughter, and a senior in high school. She had a string-bean of body with long, brunette hair piled in a fussy bun on top of her head. She was balancing a computer on her arms and standing on the other side of the coffee table, looking rather nervous.

"Sure. What's up?"

"Can you help me talk my parents into letting me study abroad like you?" Charley swooped around the table and collapsed on the couch beside her, thrusting her MacBook toward Paige.

Charley was breathing hard and chewing her bottom lip, but Paige had seen her determined look before. It was one many of her more academically inclined students wore. They had dreams, and nothing was going to stand in their way.

Paige took a deep breath. "Let's back up a minute." She glanced at the computer screen and saw a website for a university in Costa Rica. "What's your plan?"

"Here's what I'm thinking." Charley leaned in and clicked open another document. "I've put together a check list."

For the next ten minutes, Paige listened nonstop to how Charley wanted to help save the environment and the rain forests by getting her degree in plant biology. Once she had her degree, she could work on research teams or in a lab conducting statistical research related to the genetics and evolution of plants. Basically, she was singlehandedly going to save the planet.

Paige held her smile in place when she spotted several holes in Charley's ambitious plan. "That all sounds wonderful, so let's run through a couple of things. Have you ever been to Costa Rica? Is the language barrier an issue? Does the university provide housing? Will you need to work? How are you going to pay the tuition?"

Charley's intense ambition faded into a frown. "We went to Costa Rica on vacation once, but that's all."

"You might need to answer a few more questions before you take the plunge and apply. This is a big step. Costa Rica places a high degree of emphasis on literacy. Education is highly prized, and the universities are competitive. You'll need to have the grades to get in."

"I've got the grades," Charley assured her.

"Living in Costa Rica is very different from living in California. You'll probably stay in an apartment with several other students, and you won't have a car since everyone travels by bus. And the food is different. I overheard you fussing about your meal this morning. Rice, beans, fruit, and vegetables are the main cuisine. Being a picky eater could be a problem, and you don't want to get sick."

"Oh." Charley bit her lip. "I didn't think of that."

Paige studied Charley's designer jeans and name-brand T-shirt. "It sounds like a small issue, but you will also have to consider your wardrobe. Electricity is expensive in Costa Rica. You'll be doing laundry every weekend and hanging your clothes up to dry. Forget about dry-cleaning or shopping at your favorite department store. Clothes are a practical consideration, not a luxury."

"Charley, lunch is ready." Julie, Noah's oldest sister, walked into the living room, drying her hands on a kitchen towel. "We're having tuna fish sandwiches today."

"Ew, gross, Mom." Charley shivered and accepted the laptop Paige handed her. "I'll just have a bowl of cereal."

"Uh, Charley." Paige waited for the young woman to turn around. "Milk in Costa Rica is ultra-pasteurized and not refrigerated. You drink it warm."

A horrified look crossed Charley's face. "Maybe I don't want to go to Costa Rica. I'll have to think of something else. I can't drink warm milk. That's just gross."

Julie tracked Charley's movements as she swerved around her and headed into the kitchen.

"Whatever you said to my kid, thank you. I don't want to crush her dreams, but they seem to change from day to day. She's had her mind set on studying in Costa Rica for a month now. Nothing Brent or I have said could dissuade her. Especially since she's smart enough to get a scholarship and living allowance, and she'll be eighteen next month."

Paige made room for Julie to sit next to her on the couch. "I spent a year teaching in Costa Rica. It's a beautiful place, and the beaches are amazing, but after a while the traffic got to me. It would take me thirty minutes by bus to get to a school only a few miles away."

"Noah tells me you're thinking about coming back to the States."

"Maybe. That's the current plan." Paige let a smile settle into place, but she was worried. She'd looked at apartment rentals and job boards in California, and everything seemed so expensive. Part of her wondered if coming back to stay had been the right decision. Her mom was still in California, but she lived six hours south of Oakland, where she and Olivia were raised. The town was small, and she worried about the number of available jobs. Her father lived across the country in Florida.

Paige didn't have a family home anymore. If she stayed, she'd have to carve out her own place, rebuild old friendships, and create her own family. That would be hard to do alone.

"The way you handled Charley was perfect, better than any of her school counselors." Julie's expression brightened. "One of my friends runs an online college placement counseling service for students wanting to come to the States for their education and those who want to study abroad. If you like, I can give her your information."

The tension across Paige's shoulders eased by the thought of this new possibility.

"That sounds great. I love helping students make plans to achieve their dreams."

"Good." Julie paused and touched Paige's knee. "It's really good to see you again. You and Noah. The time away has changed you, but deep down it's easy to see the Paige we're so fond of."

There were so many ways Paige could interpret Julie's statement, but she chose instead to not think too hard about the possible implications.

"Come." Julie pointed toward the kitchen. "As soon as everyone is done with lunch, we're setting up to make wedding favors. Mia asked if you'd like to help."

"Of course. I'd love to." Paige tucked her computer in her bag, stashed it in her room for safekeeping, then wandered back into the kitchen.

The place was now in chaos, amid wall-to-wall people.

The bride-to-be handed her a plate. "Help yourself to the sandwiches," Mia pointed. "The fruit is over there on the counter, and there are cups and drinks on the table."

Paige filled her plate, skirted the counter, and moved toward the huge table. The kids were just finishing up, and the adults were taking over

She took a seat on the far end, setting her meal on a woven brown placemat. Mia plopped down next to her. Laughter and chatter filled the room. Instead of finding the noise and press of bodies oppressive, Paige felt cocooned in love and warmth. She hadn't felt a part of something like this in ages.

"Paige, dear," Aunt Rosa called. "It's poker night. Are you

going to join us?"

"If I remember correctly, the last time I played poker with you, I was out twenty dollars." Paige placed a napkin in her lap. "I'll pass. You're too much of a card shark for me."

Aunt Rosa laughed, her generous bosom quaking. "My girls signed up for a horseback outing this afternoon. They said they'll catch up with you later."

Warmth spread through her like sun-warmed honey. The Myers' extended family was just as kind and close as the rest of the gang. Paige enjoyed being included for the few special occasions she'd been able to attend, which included aunts, uncles, and cousins. She was pleased they still remembered her.

"Hey, babe." Alec, a wiry blond with a runner's build and round glasses that gave him a bookish air, placed a kiss on Mia's cheek and dropped into the seat next to her.

Across the kitchen, Noah plucked a bunch of grapes out of one of the many bowls. Her heart sighed. He looked so delicious in his flip-flops, cream cargo shorts, and navy T-shirt. A trickle of joy replaced the anxiety and eased her trepidations.

He did that to her. Turned sadness into happiness, uncertainty into decisiveness, fear into courage.

"All caught up with your email?" Noah slid into the seat to her left.

"Yep. Hard to believe how jammed up my inbox was after just a few days."

"Anything important?" His question was casual, but she sensed a question lurking unsaid.

"Emails from my students are always important, but they were mostly about final grades on exams, projects, and papers. They all did exceptionally well." Paige bit off the top of a carrot stick and crunched. "What have you been up to this morning?"

"Mia needed more birdseed for the wedding favors so Alec, Logan, and I ran up to the hardware store in town to get more."

"It took all three of you?"

"Well, no. Mia asked Alec to go, and Logan and I went along to lend him our support." His shifty gaze said the errand went beyond birdseed.

"The three of you went on a beer run, didn't you?"

He reached for a bottle of water. "What makes you think that?"

"Oh, the fact you won't look at me, and the grin you're trying to hide."

"I never could get away with anything around you."

She didn't know why he bothered. Noah was one of the good guys. Whatever he was up to was done to make someone happy or fix a problem. He wasn't selfish or resentful. Never had been, and there was one of the reasons she loved him.

She looked down at her hands and curled them into fists to keep them from reaching for Noah. His family had a way of sussing out a person's truth, and she couldn't let anyone guess. The awkwardness of being called out scared her.

Before she left for Europe after Olivia's death, Noah and she had a brother-sister kind of conversation. He told her then he'd never marry again, and that his heart would always belong to Olivia. He'd been speaking from the depths of his grief. Given time, feelings might change. And Noah had started dating again, yet none of the women seemed to have captured his heart the way Olivia had.

Did this mean she had a chance?

"Alec," Julie called from the kitchen, "aren't you guys supposed to be at the tux shop this afternoon?"

"Oh, crap. That's right. Finish eating, fellas. We need to

leave or we're going to be late." Alec stood and reached into his pocket for the keys. "Thanks for the reminder."

"I call shotgun," Logan yelled just before he shoved an entire quarter sandwich in his mouth.

"What are you, seven years old?" Julie threw her hands in the air. "And you wonder where our children get their bad habits."

"I guess I'll eat later." Noah winked at Paige. "Have fun playing with the birdseed." He slid his chair back under the table before heading for the front door.

That, right there, was why she adored him. There couldn't be one person on the planet who didn't like him. He was kind and clever and generous with his time. Whenever he was around his family, he was present, not tucked in some corner working on a computer all day. He was there for each person, adapting and giving each what they needed without asking for anything in return.

Even her.

That morning, he'd let her sleep in until he woke her up with a cup of freshly brewed coffee and a warm blueberry crumble muffin. He'd been so sweet, ceremoniously placing a section of paper towel on her lap, and then waiting while she adjusted her pillow to prop herself up.

He told her he was going to take the kids off Kaylee's hands for an hour to wear off some of their energy. And it worked. The younger ones staggered back into the house and took a nap, while the older ones settled in to watch a movie.

She loved watching the morning unfold. The love their family had for each member was true, authentic. No words need be spoken. What the Myers family had was real.

For the weekend, at least, she was part of that love.

She'd take it in. Store it. Reserve it for the days when she was far away from an exclusive club such as this one.

She'd hold on until it was again time to let go.

Chapter 8

*L*ogan pushed Noah aside as he shoved past him and climbed into the passenger seat, earning a hot glare from his brother. Noah tucked himself into the back seat while Alec jumped into the driver's seat and started the car.

Noah's older brother, Logan, had been mean-tempered since Noah's arrival, and it was grating on his nerves. Normally he'd ignore Logan's brutish behavior, but he didn't want it upsetting others this weekend, especially Mia.

"What's up with you, Logan?" Noah wanted to smack him upside the head, just to rile his older brother. Anything would be better than Logan's grumpy attitude and gruff, one-word answers. So far, he'd avoided joining in family activities and kept mostly to himself. "You've been a bear all weekend."

"Don't mind him." Alec drove away from the villa toward the small town a few miles from the resort. "Cindy is taking him back to court for more child support because he got a new job with an increase in pay."

"Aw, man, I'm sorry to hear that. Why didn't you tell me?" Noah clapped his brother on the shoulder sympathetically.

"It's not like I want to talk about Cindy or my problems. Why bother when you're just going to leave anyway." Logan stared out the passenger window, his profile stony.

That had to be the twentieth time someone had mentioned his absence in the past twenty-four hours. The recording needed to stop playing.

"Fine. Don't talk to me." He glazed toward Alec. "So... what's up with John?" He asked hoping Alec would do his usual and fill him in on all the family dynamics he'd missed, since no one else seemed compelled to share the details during family phone calls or video chats. "Kaylee keeps making excuses for why her husband's not here."

Alec met his gaze in the rearview mirror. "They're good, as far as I know."

"Nothing's wrong between them," Logan finally said. "They're solid, a team, just like Mom and Dad. John used all his personal time after his paternity leave expired to stay home with Max for the first few months, so he's short on vacation time. He'll be up for the wedding day after tomorrow."

If everything was fine between Kaylee and John, why was Logan still annoyed? Then Noah realized his brother was civil to everyone else, for the most part. His bad-tempered mood and sharp words seemed to be directed only at him.

There was only one thing it could be.

"Logan, if you're still angry at me for not coming home for Dad's funeral, just say it. I'm tired of tiptoeing around you." Noah folded his arms, steeling himself for his brother's response.

"Fine. I'm pissed you didn't come home." Logan pounded the side of his fist against the car window, fortunately not hard enough to break it. "There. I said it."

"Dude, I can't fix what's in the past, and you know I don't do funerals." Noah's hands curled into fists. "I offered to come home afterwards, but Mom said to wait, something about possibly selling the house, and figuring out what she wanted to do next."

"Funerals are for the living, not the dead. We should have buried Dad together." Logan's voice was raspy. "Mom needed you. We all needed you."

"I talked to Mom. She was okay with me staying in London. Plus, money was tight." Every objection he gave for not attending his father's funeral after his heart gave out was a pathetic excuse to cover up the truth. Ever since burying his twenty-four-year-old wife, he didn't have the strength to say goodbye to anyone else.

"That was a bull crap excuse, and you know it." Logan turned and sneered over one shoulder. "I offered to buy your plane ticket to come home. I needed you here. Just like you needed us when Olivia died."

So that was it.

Logan always had been a scorekeeper. If he shared his Halloween candy, he expected others to share their Easter candy. If he let Noah pick what movie they went to, the next time Logan got to pick. Before Noah got his driver's license, if Logan drove him to a friend's house, Noah could expect to be charged for the exact amount of gas the trip consumed.

He hadn't realized Logan was waiting to collect on a debt incurred sixteen years ago. Resentment and frustration warred in his belly, an unsettling hot and cold mix, that *everything* somehow came back to Olivia. He'd left home to escape, yet Olivia had him tethered to a past he couldn't seem to free himself from.

"I'm sorry, Logan. I truly am sorry I wasn't there when you needed me." His heavy sigh filled the interior of the car.

"I'm not perfect. But I do my best to be a good man. A good brother. A good friend."

"That's what makes you acting like a martyr so frustrating." Logan's voice was thick. "You are a good man. But you're only half a man. The other half is stuck in the past with Olivia. When are you going to let it go? Olivia's been gone sixteen years, but she's still controlling your life. Everything you do is because of what happened."

"Don't go there." A flash of anger boiled and exploded. He gripped the back of Logan's seat with white-knuckled fists. "You know *nothing* about what I went through with her."

"Just smoke and mirrors, buddy. Deflect the truth with accusations no one will call you on." Logan twisted in his seat, his dark eyes sad, jaw no longer clenched with anger. "We know what you went through. We saw it every day when we came to visit you and Olivia or bring a meal or take a turn driving you both to medical appointments. We heard you crying at night. We saw the desperation each time she took a turn for the worse. You gave up college so you could marry Olivia and spend what little time remained with her. You gave her everything, Noah. But the problem is, you're still sacrificing your life for her."

Noah sat back, stunned by his brother's insights. Everything Logan said was true, but the way he said it made Noah sound selfish.

"Olivia was twenty-four. She had her whole life in front of her, and the cancer just ate away at her, day by day by day, and there was nothing I could do." Noah shook his head. How did such tragedy not change a man and scar his soul forever?

"Sometimes things happen in life we can't control." Logan's harsh laugh held no humor. "Like when your wife divorces you and takes your kids away. You do what you can and learn to cope. No one could save Olivia, so you did what you could. That has to be enough. What do you think she'd say if she saw you living this half existence? She'd want you to move on. You and Paige."

"What about Paige?" He wanted to punch his brother for bringing Paige into the conversation, but curiosity made him hold off.

"See? That's what I'm talking about. You're blind." Logan snorted. "Alec, help me out here."

"Leave me out of this one." Alec shook his head. "I'm not part of the family yet, and I don't want Mia upset because I inflamed an argument between her brothers."

"Chicken," Logan huffed.

"Let's get back on track here." Now Logan wasn't needling him, Noah was willing to continue the dialogue. "What about Paige?"

"Paige was gone before the grass grew back on Olivia's grave. Not that I blame her. First, she loses her sister, then her parents split up." Logan adjusted the A/C and rested his arm on the console between the seats. "I don't know which one of you is more pathetic. Both of you are always on the move, thinking you can outrun the past or dodge the pain. If there's one thing I learned since Cindy walked out, at the end of the day, you're still stuck with yourself and everything inside."

"Armchair psychology from a guy who makes a living writing code." Noah was being defensive because his brother hit a sore spot, one he didn't like being poked.

"It doesn't take a degree to see the truth when it's right in front of you." Logan stared ahead as if directing his comments to Alec instead of Noah. "Paige has worshipped the ground you walk on since she was old enough to realize the difference between boys and girls. But since her sister loved you, she never said a word. Paige would never have done anything to hurt Olivia. In fact, everyone went to great extremes to make sure Olivia had anything and everything she wanted. I'm not saying Olivia played the C-card, but did you ever stop to consider maybe you stayed with her, even married her, more out of loyalty than love?"

"That's total—" Noah shouted then stopped because Alec slowed the car and pulled over to the side of the road.

"Finish this," Alec said tightly, "so we can get to the tux shop without this drama continuing to simmer all weekend."

"Fine." Logan twisted in the passenger seat, eyes blazing. "Paige is still in love with you, dumbass. Always has been, probably always will be. Now, she's your wedding *date*. She's here, doing her best to hide her feelings for you, and you're using her to avoid pressure from Mom and our sisters to settle down. Did you ever consider how your actions make Paige feel?"

"She's my sister-in-law, if you haven't forgotten." Noah hurled the fact at Logan the same way he reminded himself of it every time he felt his body and heart yearning for Paige, believing it was only because he missed Olivia. He would never use Paige in that way…ever.

This was Paige they were talking about. She'd always been like a sister to him. When Olivia died, the bond developed into a friendship that stood on its own merits.

"And for that reason, she'll never reveal her feelings," Logan stated flatly. "She'd consider it a betrayal of the love between you and Olivia. If either of you has a genuine desire to let go of the past, you'll have to decide how you feel about each other and confront the issue. She's trapped not only by her grief over losing her sister, but the hopelessness of loving a man who's devoted to a ghost."

Logan threw down the challenge the same way he'd goaded Noah into trying out for the football team when he didn't think he was good enough. His older brother was always coaxing him in a direction he thought fitting, even if at the time Noah didn't agree.

"You've been watching too much Dr. Phil." Noah did his best to lighten the mood and redirect the conversation. "Paige is at a crossroads in her life which has nothing to do with me. Besides, she's considering staying in California, and I'm headed back to Singapore when the wedding is over."

"Good for Paige." Logan nodded. "Maybe you should take a page from her playbook. Mom isn't getting any younger, and you barely know your nieces and nephews. And besides, you work remotely, so it's not like you'd jeopardize your career by moving back."

The silence in the car was deafening. Logan tended to stew about things, but when the floodgates opened, everything came pouring out.

"Logan, you done spouting your opinions?"

"Yeah, I'm done. Not that saying anything does any good. Your head's as thick as a coconut."

"Good thing I've got a thick head since you like taking swings at me from time to time." Noah thumped the back of Alec's seat. "Let's go. I've had enough psychoanalysis from Dr. Freud here."

Paige was his sister-in-law. His friend. His anchor. He needed her to be that safe person. He needed her to be that one person he didn't have to keep at arm's length to avoid being hurt.

But he couldn't deny there was something between them. He'd sensed it the moment he laid eyes on her at the airport. For years, they'd kept their precious bond from fraying through texts and video calls. Distance made things easy to hide. Like how much he needed her and relied on her for comfort and connection. Maybe she'd used distance to hide her feelings for him. He let the revelation sink in.

If Paige wanted more than friendship, it wasn't fair to

string her along. He needed to figure out how he felt about her. Talk to her.

Damn it all. This trip had already been complicated, and now it was more so.

Sometimes he hated Logan for always being right.

Chapter 9

*D*espite the previous night's sleep, Paige felt the jet lag catching up with her. Her shoulders were stiff, and she was having trouble focusing. Her fingers hurt from boxing up the cute packages of birdseed meant to shower the newlyweds after they completed their exchange of vows.

As much as she longed for a nap, she was unwilling to leave the table where all the Myers women were gathered. For the past three hours, they'd chatted and laughed and traipsed down memory lane, sharing familiar stories, some including Paige, and anecdotes she'd never heard before. She was surprised to find the sometimes stoic and introverted Julie told the best stories.

The one Julie told about Noah dressing the Thanksgiving turkey in sunglasses and a bow tie was one she would never forget. The family adored pranks, but only those delivered in good fun.

Paige loved being part of this loud, affectionate group. Unlike her parents, who never discussed anything the least bit improper or uncomfortable, Noah's parents had always encouraged open, honest communication. When one of their children messed up, whether it was Julie getting pregnant her senior year of high school or Logan streaking nude across the beach on spring break, they knew their parents still loved and supported them…all while holding them responsible for the consequences of their actions.

Paige's kinship with her parents was more tenuous. She and her mom were closer than they'd been in years, but there was still a degree of formality between them, and she suspected the physical distance between them probably had a lot to do with their strained relationship. Moving back to California would allow them to spend time together, get reacquainted, and rebuild from the wreckage of their lives.

Her father had remarried ten years ago and seemed content to talk a few times a year. Hearing Mrs. Myers and Mia talk about how much they missed Mr. Myers and wished he could be a part of the wedding made Paige realize how lucky she was because her father was still alive. Doing nothing to redeem their father-daughter relationship made her feel lazy and ungrateful. She wasn't sure how to reach out to her dad, but had added it to her list of issues needing a resolution.

In a way, she was jealous that Noah had had an entire family to grieve with. It saddened her when he decided to struggle on his own, ignore the hurt, and run from the pain, leaving behind a confused family who didn't know how to help.

But she knew what he needed. He needed her to be on the other end of the line when he'd had too many drinks or just broke up with a woman who looked like Olivia.

Deep in thought, she didn't notice the chatter quiet until she saw a tub of red licorice appear in front of her.

"My favorite!" She grabbed for the plastic container and hugged the bucket to her chest. She searched behind her for the delivery person and discovered Noah with a delighted look on his face. "What is this for?"

"I promised you rest and relaxation, and you've been working all day." Noah came around the end of the table, into her line of vision. Logan and Alec entered behind him.

"This is totally relaxing." She glanced around at all the strong, wonderful women she could spend a lifetime with and never get bored. "No lesson plans. No quizzes or exams. No schedule to keep. It's just what I needed."

"Are you going to share?" Noah asked noting she had not released her possessive grip on the candy.

Her gaze swept around the table. "It depends."

"On what?" Mia took the bait.

"Since you're all into telling stories, I would like for each of you to tell me an embarrassing story about Noah." She met his grin with one of her own. "I know a lot of them, but I keep hearing new ones about the rest of the family. There have to be some gems I haven't heard yet."

"Give me that back." Noah reached, but she held the container out of his reach.

"Who's first?" She opened the candy and waggled it, sending out the sweet, fruity strawberry scent.

"Aunt Rosa, you should tell Paige the cow story," Kaylee suggested.

Noah groaned.

"Yes. The cow story. I don't know that one." Paige laughed while Noah slumped down beside her in the only open chair at the end of the table.

"The little snot," Aunt Rosa began. "We didn't have a big spread, just a couple of horses, a cow, and some chickens. Noah was about four or five, and Julie was supposed to be watching him and the other young kids. Noah snuck off into the pasture, climbed up onto a tree stump, and somehow got himself situated on Petunia, our cow. She was old and fat, and slow and gentle as can be, but when I saw him riding around on her back, I screamed like a crazy lady. If something had happened to him, Bernice would have wrung my neck."

Rosa looked at her sister-in-law, who frowned in mock anger, then went on. "When I hollered, Noah toppled off Petunia's back. Nearly gave me a heart attack." She clapped a hand over her chest, remembering. "I ran to the middle of the field only to find him lying there laughing."

"Tell Paige the best part," Logan snickered.

"Oh...well...when he fell, he landed in a fresh cow patty." Rosa shuddered as she remembered the image. "He was covered with cow poop."

"Oh, no!" Paige covered her mouth, her hand the only thing that was holding back the laughter bubbling inside. "What happened next?"

"My Aunt embarrassed the crap out of me is what happened next." Noah threw a fond look at Rosa. "Pun intended."

She covered her mouth to hide her laughter, but then saw everyone else's shoulders were shaking, their eyes sparkling with laughter.

"You deserved what you got. I made you strip down to your skin in the barn," Rosa continued, "and I hosed you off."

"The worst part was my siblings watching this all happen." Noah grimaced.

"They didn't see anything," Rosa said, waving a dismissive hand. "I wrapped you in a horse blanket and made you go inside to take a proper shower."

"Oh, no." Paige pointed at Noah. "I know that look. What did you do?" she accused, knowing whatever happened, the outcome would be memorable.

"What any young boy would do." His eyes gleamed with remembered mischief. "I went into the house, grabbed a handful of chocolate chip cookies, and snuck out the back door."

"You didn't."

"Oh, yes, he did," his mother added. "We'd just gotten back from a trip into town for groceries, and it took us hours to find him. Scared me and Henry to death."

"You should tell Paige the one about the flowers." Julie picked up the birdseed bag to measure out a portion for the next wedding favor she was assembling.

"Oh, that's a good one." Mia's shoulders shook with laughter. "It was so good, Noah didn't even get into trouble for stealing all Mom's garden flowers."

"I didn't steal them," Noah protested. "I gave them to the neighbors."

Bernice's face softened as she gathered the details of the memory. "Every night, around the dinner table, the kids would share one thing they learned or experienced during the day. One of the girls, I don't remember which one, talked about the May Day tradition of placing paper baskets with spring flowers on people's doorsteps, ringing the doorbell, and running away so the giver remains secret."

Paige looked at Noah. "I bet he liked the idea of ringing the doorbell and running."

"He did." Bernice's smile expressed love and tolerance for her son's antics. "He liked it so much, he picked every single one of the flowers in my garden to make May Day bouquets. I had no idea what was going on until I started getting calls from neighbors, saying how sweet my boy was and how much the flowers brightened their day." She wagged her finger at him. "I should have grounded you for a month."

"Yes, you should have," Kaylee agreed from the doorway, where she was bouncing Max, who just woke up from a nap. "He always got away with stuff the rest of us never could."

A childish shriek from the living room area of the villa interrupted the storytelling.

"That's one of mine." Kaylee handed Max to Logan and darted out of the room, shouting a disapproving, "What happened?"

There was murmured conversation, then Kaylee ushered Ben, Luke, and James into the kitchen. She held up a mangled white silk pillow and glared, waiting for a confession. "Boys!"

"We were playing football." Ben, Julie and Brent's fifteen-year-old, hung his head. "Luke and James were fighting over the pillow in the end zone, and the thing came apart."

The younger two, Kaylee's eleven- and nine-year-old sons, peeked at Ben and mimicked his shameful pose—heads down, worried eyes peeking up.

"Sorry, Aunt Mia," all three intoned.

"My ring pillow." Mia gasped, tears glimmering in her eyes.

Paige was up and out of her chair in an instant. "No worries. If there's a fabric store nearby, I can pick up some silk and lace and make a new one in time for the wedding."

Mia reached for the ruined pillow. "Are you sure?"

"It won't be as fancy as this one but, depending on what kind of lace is available, I might be able to come close. Clothes are expensive in some of the places I lived, so I learned how to mend and hem." Paige wrapped an arm around Mia's shoulders. "It won't take me long to whip up a new one." Paige picked up the bucket of licorice and offered Mia a stick. "Have one. It'll help you feel better."

The boys' eyes lit up. "Can we have some candy?"

"No!" the adults roared simultaneously.

Paige laughed as the villa's front door opened, and noisy footsteps and laughter invaded the kitchen. It was Brent, Charley, and Riley, back from a swim in the resort's pool.

"Uh-oh." Brent looked around, taking in the scene. "Who's in trouble?"

"Your son and nephews," Julie said. "They got a bit rambunctious and destroyed Mia's ring pillow while trying for a touchdown. I think a ten-mile hike in full gear is just the thing to burn off their energy."

"What's full gear?" James whispered loudly to his older brother, eyes wide with dread.

"My mom keeps threatening to send me away to boot camp. Full gear is what the military guys wear, including a huge backpack. She's just trying to scare us." Ben pulled a thin canvas wallet out of the side pocket of his cargo shorts and handed Paige a twenty. "My spending money for this weekend, but you can use it to buy the supplies to replace Aunt Mia's pillow."

Mia sniffled, then smiled, obviously touched by her nephew's gesture. She turned to Alec. "How about you guys take the boys down to the stables? See if Cade Foster, the stable director, is around. Maybe the boys can muck out a few stalls for penance. If not, take them out for a horseback ride. Us girls can finish up the wedding favors and start getting ready for dinner."

"Come on." Noah curved his arm loosely around Paige's shoulder. "There has to be a fabric store nearby."

Her body tingled as she savored the warmth of his skin through the thin fabric of her T-shirt and the lingering scent of the resort's handmade soaps provided for guests. He'd chosen Pacific Woodlands. She could tell because it had a strong pine and cedar scent compared to Ocean Breeze, her selection, which leaned more toward the fresh eucalyptus aroma. Noah's scent made her want to snuggle in and get a good whiff.

Julie nodded toward a small side table. "Your rental car keys are over there."

"I'm glad Brent's here. I'll have time this weekend to get better acquainted," Paige said. "I only met him once or twice before…I left."

Noah's arm tightened around her, becoming more of an embrace. He understood how a throwaway comment could suddenly trigger a landslide of emotions.

The group's conversation and activity eddied around them like a stream coursing around a small island. Paige felt her connection to Noah strengthen. The two of them were bound by their memories and grief, but today there was something more. Something she had a hard time describing but felt like safety and security and permanence no amount of change could undermine.

Could they share something more than friendship? Was Noah ready to make room in his heart for someone new? Or was it just her imagination?

One thing was clear. After listening to all the stories about Noah and his antics, it confirmed that he was a good man, and she was more in love than ever.

Now all she needed to do was get him to love her back.

And she had the perfect plan: —to cinch up her bra straps, tell him about her feelings, and hope he didn't jump into a car and race to the nearest airport.

Chapter 10

*N*oah stared at the bedroom ceiling, doing his best to sleep, but his mind wouldn't shut off. The conversation with Logan kept rolling around in his head, and memories of a young Paige handing him a homemade Valentine's Day card, baking him a birthday cupcake, and asking for a picture with him on prom night when he was wearing a tux came to mind. At the time he'd believed it was just Olivia's kid sister being nice to her older sis's boyfriend.

But what if it had been more?

"Paige?" He whispered her name, and then held his breath to listen for movement from the bunk below "Are you awake?"

He was answered by a loud sigh.

"Jet lag sucks. It'll take a week to even out my sleep routine." She shifted on the mattress, a slight tremor moving through the bedframe. "That explains why I'm still awake, but what about you?"

"I've been thinking." He linked his fingers behind his head, cushioned by the pillow beneath.

"About the website you're supposed to be working on? I noticed you haven't put in any time on it since I arrived."

"No, but I made excellent progress last week. It's almost done." He listened to Paige's rhythmic breathing in the silence. "I was thinking about what happened with Olivia. I've never really talked about it with anyone. My family never fully understood, and since then," he took a deep breath, "well, I just locked it away."

"Yeah, me, too. It's easy when you keep so busy you don't have time to think."

He leaned over the edge of the bunk, searching for her face in the moonlight, but all he saw were shadows. "Would you be up for talking about it?"

"Is there ice cream in the freezer?"

He choked off a laugh. "I hid the chocolate chunk with caramel and toffee in the back. Even the Myers family can't go through four quarts of ice cream in a single evening."

"Let's see if there's any left." She threw back the covers, scrambled out of bed, and pulled on her bathrobe.

He climbed down the ladder, careful to avoid hitting his head on the ceiling.

Paige handed him the sweatshirt he'd tossed over the back of a chair. "I forgot how chilly it gets along the coast, even in June."

Impulsively, he took her hand and led her out of the bedroom. They crept past closed bedroom doors, careful not to disturb the rest of the family.

In the kitchen, he dropped her hand and dug around in the freezer for the hidden tub.

"Score." He held up the carton for her to see.

"I'll get the bowls." She moved toward the cupboard.

"Do we need them?" He held up two spoons.

"Good point."

Instead of heading for the kitchen table, she padded out

to the living room, where they sat side by side on the couch, the room illuminated by sufficient moonlight that lamps weren't needed

Noah handed her a spoon and pulled the lid off the ice cream carton. Each took a spoonful before he finally spoke. "Olivia's death had such an impact on so many lives."

"You don't need to tell me that." Paige scooped an oversized wad of ice cream into her mouth, swallowing so fast Noah doubted she even tasted it. He'd bet a hundred bucks she just gave herself an ice cream headache. But the ice cream freeze wasn't about indulging in the carbs, or the satisfaction of a sugar high. He got why she kept reaching again and again for another scoop—it was a way to avoid responding to his statement. "Those last few months of her life were so hard, but they passed so quickly. Everyone was determined to make the most of the time she had left. Dad brought her fresh flowers every day."

"Daisies." Noah gulped around the knot in his throat. "I remember."

"Mom cooked all her favorite foods, even though Olivia didn't have much of an appetite." Sadness tinged Paige's voice. "And then you proposed. She was so happy."

"And you sacrificed your senior year of high school to help take care of her." Noah let the ice cream melt in his mouth.

"It wasn't about taking care of her," Paige said softly. "It was about claiming every single minute with her before…."

Noah jammed his spoon into the ice cream, the creamy sweetness now sour on his tongue. After he and Olivia were married, he moved in with the Weavers so they wouldn't be robbed of time with their daughter.

"She died so quickly. Once she took a turn for the worse, it was a few short weeks, and then she was gone," he said.

"I think that's what Olivia wanted." Paige toyed with her

spoon, now licked clean. "When she woke up on her last day, I swear it was as if she was herself again. She was alert, her face had color, her eyes were bright. She thanked me for being a great little sister and made me promise to live my life to the fullest. It was like she knew the end was near."

"Then there was the funeral." He leaned his head back against the couch. "It seemed like everyone we'd ever known was there. I have flashes of memories, but it's mostly a blur."

"The next month was a blur for me," Paige murmured. "Dad moved out two weeks after the funeral. It was supposed to be temporary, but you know what happened. Mom wandered around the house like a lost soul. She would sit in Olivia's room for hours, holding one of her stuffed animals or a cheerleading sweater, staring into space.

"And I felt so helpless. For as long as I could remember, everything was about Olivia. In the beginning, it was because she was so popular and active at school and in the community. Later it was because of her cancer."

Her voice caught as she choked back a sob. "Even after Olivia died, everything was still about her."

"Is that why you left?" Noah thought Paige had fled because of grief. "Were you jealous of Olivia?"

She didn't answer.

"It doesn't make you a bad person if you were." Noah tried to imagine what it had been like for Paige, first overshadowed by Olivia's accomplishments and how well-loved she was in their community, and then overlooked by everyone, including him and her parents, because of the horrible cancer diagnosis.

"I never told anyone," he said, "but I was furious with Olivia when she died. One night I went out to the cemetery with a baseball bat. I was so angry, all I could think of was destroying her headstone. Seeing her name and those dates carved into stone made it real." He closed his eyes, trying to keep images of that dark night at bay. He'd actually struck the gray marble twice before collapsing in front of it, sobbing so hard he couldn't breathe.

"I haven't been back to the cemetery since the funeral." Paige's admission was heavy with remorse.

"We've both been on the run for years, haven't we?" Noah found her hand and twined their fingers together. "My mom and sisters kept encouraging me to talk about my feelings. Mia said I needed grief counseling. Dad was more understanding. Sometimes we'd take off in his Mustang and just drive. No destination. No conversation. Just the road and peace and quiet. When my dad died a few years back, all those same feelings came rushing back. I felt guilty about not coming back home more often to see him and the rest of the family. That's partly why I didn't come back for his funeral. I was ashamed."

"Your family loves you, Noah, no matter what. They try to help the best they know how." She squeezed his hand.

"I know. I can't believe how angry I got. It wasn't Olivia's fault she died, but there was no one else to blame. Most days I just wanted to hit something, and one day I did. I hit Logan."

Paige sucked in a breath, her eyes wide. "I didn't know that."

"Yep. I feel bad about it to this day, but you know Logan. Always pushing. He implied the only reason I stayed with Olivia and asked her to marry me was because she was sick."

"He didn't!" Paige gasped.

"He did. Logan has no filter, which is what probably cost him his marriage." Noah's heart beat painfully against his sternum.

Another secret he'd never revealed was he was afraid there was some truth in Logan's allegation. He and Olivia had been childhood sweethearts. They might have gotten married one day, but when her cancer returned, it forced the decision. Noah had planned to attend college to pursue a career as an athletic coach at the university or pro level, but the dream would require leaving Olivia, and what kind of asshole abandoned his girlfriend when she was battling cancer?

"Do you think Logan was right?" Her voice trembled. "Maybe if the cancer hadn't rushed you two into marriage you might have fallen for… for someone else?"

The dreaded question, impossible to answer.

"Asking the what-if questions can drive you crazy." He let out a stiff laugh. "I have firsthand experience with this. What if Olivia survived? What if I didn't ask her to marry me? What if I went off to college and left her behind? What if I'd stayed here and dealt with the grief? Would I have healed enough for a real relationship instead of this dating merry-go-round I'm on?"

Paige let go of a hefty sigh. "Yeah, I have a few of my own what-ifs."

Paige is still in love with you. Always has been, probably always will be. Logan's bold statement came back to Noah, loud and clear and mocking.

"Losing my twenty-four-year-old wife to cancer explains my emotional dysfunctionality," Noah said. "What's your excuse?"

"What do you mean?"

"Why are you thirty-four and still single?" Noah wanted to grip her hand tighter, as if to hold onto her for himself. "You're beautiful, smart, independent, adventurous. I'm sure you've met all kinds of interesting men in your travels."

"None of them are the one. It's also hard to build anything permanent when you move every couple of years." She carefully withdrew her hand. "I'm not sure this is the right time for this conversation. It's late...or early. We should get some sleep."

"Oh, no you don't. You don't get off that easy. It's your turn to spill."

"Maybe agreeing to attend Mia's wedding together was a mistake."

His breathing stopped for a second. "Why do you think it's a mistake?"

"I'm sure every time you see me you think of Olivia. I'm triggering old memories and bringing up all those horrible feelings. That must be why you can't sleep. I remind you of her."

"I guess that's true in a way." He curled his fingers into his palm. "But there are good memories. And the new memories don't include Olivia."

"What new memories?" She pulled at the belt of her robe, cinching it tighter until the strands of fabric were stretched to the max.

He scratched his forehead. "Like the time I called you when I was so drunk I didn't know where I was. You stayed up with me until my roommate found me outside our favorite pub in London."

"It was Olivia's birthday. Not a good example."

"I know." He snapped his fingers. "What about the time I called to get your help with an article I was writing?"

"That doesn't count either." She sighed wearily. "You were writing a blog post about the ten things you learned after losing a loved one. No one in your family had died, so I assume you were writing about Olivia."

"Has the word jerk vanished from my forehead yet?" He leaned in closer. "If I were you, I'd have kicked my butt to the curb a long time ago. Why haven't you?"

"Because you understand what it feels like to be abandoned."

"Is that part of why you haven't married? You're afraid the guy will bail on you like your parents did?" He swallowed around a lump in his throat. "Like Olivia did?"

"There are lots of reasons. My independence. Moving every couple of years. Not meeting the right guy." Paige ducked her head and shoved the loose tumble of curls behind her ear. "Not wanting to put someone through what you endured while watching the cancer take Olivia."

"Paige, everyone dies." He wanted to take her hand again but resisted the urge. "It's rare for people to die as young as Olivia, though."

"My chances are higher than average." Her voice was faint in the nighttime silence.

He let out a long, slow whistle. "You believe since Olivia got cancer, you will too."

"You know our family history. My mom had cancer, and so did my grandma. My mom survived, but the Big C took my grandmother and sister. Statistically, I'm at risk. I had a DNA test done to reassure myself, but even those results weren't enough to put my worries to rest. Cancer is so unpredictable. When Olivia went into remission the first time, I thought she was cured. I discovered that's not how it works."

"Living with the assumption the cancer could strike at any moment would be like living with a bomb strapped to your chest. A load of stress added onto an already stressful life." He looked at her, not knowing whether to be admiring, or irritated. She'd gone down a slippery slope.

Her confession made him realize how many layers and nuances there were to grief. Coming back for the wedding, returning to the area where he grew up, spending time with nieces and nephews he barely knew, but most of all seeing Paige again had his head—and heart—spinning.

He'd expected the guilt and sadness, but not the part

about becoming self-aware. He'd been looking forward to seeing Paige because she was the only person who understood what he was going through without them exchanging a single word,. She didn't tell him enough time had passed, and he should be this or that—married, settled down, bouncing a child or three on his knee. She didn't judge, but most important, she didn't try to fix him. She was pure gold from where he was sitting.

He wanted Paige at the wedding for purely selfish reasons. Her empathy offered a respite from friends and family who had the best of intentions when offering advice but didn't have a clue what it was like to lose a wife at twenty-four.

What blindsided him was Logan's position that Paige was in love with him...and had been for years.

He'd never thought of her in that way...or had he?

Sitting next to her on the sofa, not touching, but close enough to feel the warmth of her skin and smell the floral scent of her shampoo, Noah felt the pull of something very much like desire. He and Paige had held hands in the past, shared companionable silences, and openly discussed their feelings for Olivia and her death.

What lay between them now was different. There was a subtle, not unpleasant, tension, and every nerve in his body was attuned to Paige—the combined scents of laundry soap, shampoo, and perfume, the rhythmic rise and fall of her breasts, the barely audible whisper of her breathing, and the solid, firm body just a breath from his.

And beyond the physical awareness of a man for a woman waited an emotional need he was afraid to examine too closely.

"How are you feeling now?" he asked, not sure what else to say.

"When my thirtieth birthday checkup came back clean, I thought it time to stop holding my breath."

"Holding your breath isn't good." He angled the tub of ice cream her way. "And here I thought I'd cornered the market on feeling scared about the future."

"We're both a mess." She dug out a small bite with her spoon.

"That's why we're perfect for each other." From the corner of his eye, he saw the spoon freeze in mid-air before she slowly lowered it back to the carton.

The warm pleasure triggered by her proximity chilled while he considered the subtext of the simple phrase. He hadn't meant to imply anything, except in light of Logan's assessment of her feelings for him, suggesting they were a perfect match opened all kinds of possibilities. "Um, you know what I mean."

Logan was right. How had he been so blind? The way she leaned in, the way she listened, the way she laughed even when his jokes weren't all that funny…Paige liked him. Really liked him. Way past the ordinary brother-in-law way. And the truth was, Paige could be his perfect match.

She liked to travel. Spontaneous was her middle name. She loved to watch scary thriller movies and eat buttered popcorn. He could name several dozen more things, but now his heart had beat so loud that his head finally heard what it'd been saying for years.

Paige was the one he'd been waiting for, and she'd been right in front of him all this time.

He set the ice cream on the coffee table and reached for her hand. "Talk to me. Tell me what I've been missing." He searched her eyes. When she tried to pull away, his grip tightened. "Please," he begged.

"It doesn't matter."

"What doesn't matter?" He desperately wanted her to open up, but it wasn't fair if he wasn't willing to do the same. "Paige, I'm feeling and thinking things about you I've never considered before. I'm not saying they weren't there, but I've never allowed myself to think of you in any way other than my sister-in-law."

"It's probably the pressure of family. Being with them. Seeing me. Remembering…" She hunched her shoulders. "It's sparking all kinds of crazy emotions."

"I agree, it seems a little crazy." He wanted to put his arm around her shoulders, but it was no longer a simple, friendly gesture of reassurance, so he resisted the urge. "Crazy it never dawned on me why I keep reaching out to you, and why you're so important to me. I kept telling myself it was because of our connection to Olivia, but after the past couple of days…I don't think that's why."

"You're not pulling any punches, are you?" She looked up at him through her lashes. "Well, if you are taking jabs, here's one for you."

She sighed, the pause making Noah feel as if he dangled over the edge of a cliff, ready to fall to his death unless Paige pulled him back onto solid ground.

"I've had a crush on you for as long as I can remember. I fell in love with you the day you decided to stay after Olivia told you about her terminal diagnosis. You didn't have to. You could have left. But you didn't. I guess I'm still in love with you because there's no one else in the world I can talk to the way I can talk to you. But there's always been one problem."

"Olivia." He released the breath he'd been holding.

"No." Her voice quaked. "It's your heart. The day Olivia died, you closed off your heart and haven't let anyone in since. It's like you're afraid to love anyone again."

A chill ran down his spine, and he shivered. "You've noticed that, huh?"

"Everyone has. Your family is worried about you, each in their own way."

"They were talking about me?" He turned to see her reaction.

"Only because they care."

Another stab of guilt. His mother and siblings had more important things to worry about than him. They had kids to raise and spouses to support. "I'd better do something to fix this."

"Good idea. Do it now, while you can." Paige's gaze met his. "That's why I finally told you how I feel. I don't know when I'll have another chance, and for the first time in sixteen years, I'm ready to face life, my feelings, even the past. I don't want to spend the next sixteen, or twenty, or fifty years missing out because of regrets and guilt over something I can't change."

"First things first." He reached for her hand. "Let's make this official. Oh, my beautiful Paige Weaver, would you do me the honor of being my date for my sister's wedding?"

"I'm already going to your sister's wedding." She tried to pull her hand away, but he held on.

"Yes, as my friend. I want you to go as my real date. No more pretending."

Her face went through a kaleidoscope of emotions, uncertainty shifting to disbelief shifting to hope shifting to amazement.

He didn't want her to overthink the question. All sorts of things went wrong when women thought too much. "Is that a yes?"

"You're asking me out on a date?"

"If a wedding date is too soon, I can wake you up early and find a place where we can have a quiet breakfast."

"I don't know—"

"Oh, you're killing me." He punched a fist to his heart. He

pushed up off the couch and knelt on the floor. "Please, Paige. Say yes."

"I planned to say yes, but not to breakfast out. I have a ring pillow to make, and I promised to help with the kids. Logan's two are arriving midmorning. That's nine youngsters to manage. But," the smile on her face blossomed, "I do like a man on his knees."

A wealth of satisfaction exploded and made his whole body tingle with possibilities. "So, you'll be my date?"

"Yes, I'll be your date."

"Oh, thank God." Mia shuffled into the living room, a blanket wrapped around her shoulders. "I wanted some ice cream but didn't want to interrupt." She picked up the carton on the table. "Scootch over."

Paige's cheeks were red, visible even in the dim light. Siblings are really, really good at embarrassing each other, Noah thought.

"It's about time you wised up." Mia snuggled in next to Noah. "Julie owes me ten bucks."

"Wised up in regard to what, exactly?" He eyed his sister warily.

"You and Paige. Perfect match. More than friends. Your real date for the wedding." Mia raised her brows in exaggerated disbelief at how dense she considered him to be. "I always thought you two were meant for each other."

"Sis, aren't you getting ahead of yourself?" Noah felt like a burglar caught in the glare of a police spotlight. He and Paige hadn't yet begun to explore the possibility of something between them, and already, his family—Mia, at least—was putting herself in the middle of things. "I just asked Paige out for our first date."

"Dates are overrated." She pointed with her spoon. "Communicating. Now, that's where it's at. You two have been talking to each other for how many years? Keep talking. Just make sure you're talking about the important stuff."

"Geez," a dose of irritation filled Noah's voice. "I long for the day my siblings aren't telling me what to do."

"Don't wish for your siblings to stop caring," Paige said.

He and Mia turned her way.

"I adore you both," Paige said. "You're nuts, but you're good nuts, so please remember to appreciate one another. As irritating as you are to each other, you at least have someone. I miss my sister every day. There is not a day that goes by I don't wish she was still here. I wish my mom and dad weren't so swallowed up by their hurt. I wish…" Paige looked up and shrugged. "Never mind. Too many carbs." She held up her spoon. "I must have gotten a sugar rush."

"You've got family. We're your family." Mia placed her head on Paige's shoulder. "And you're right. We need to be grateful we have each other. Thanks for the reminder."

Noah's chest tightened and then relaxed, for right then, in that moment, he couldn't hold the doors to his heart closed any longer. Paige and Mia had thrust them wide open.

Fear dribbled in until he saw the look on Paige's face. Her fingers tightened around his.

She knew what he was feeling.

But could he open up enough to hold onto her?

He wasn't sure he had the all-sacrificing kind of love in him anymore—and Paige deserved nothing less.

Chapter 11

*P*aige awoke to a pair of wide black and white plastic eyes staring at her.

"Pokey wants to give you a kiss." Emma touched her stuffed animal to Paige's face.

Paige squeezed her eyes shut and pressed her face into the pillow before rolling to a sitting position and holding a quiet finger to her lips.

"Uncle Noah is still sleeping," she whispered while she turned Emma toward the door, and slid her feet into slippers, and grabbed her robe. She staggered down the hall after the six-year-old, grateful for the smell of fresh brewed coffee wafting her way. She was grateful for the busy day ahead. The crammed schedule would prevent her from thinking too much about Noah, or the conversation they had last night. She needed all the caffeine she could manage to pour into her veins.

Kaylee was at the table setting out boxes of cereal. "Please tell me she didn't," she stopped and propped her hands on her hips with a stern look.

Paige nodded. "She did. But it's okay. I needed to get up to finish the ring pillow. I still have to sew on the ribbon and lace, but it's almost finished."

"Mia will be relieved. I don't think she's slept much in the past two days, and this morning she's already up and gone. She said something about running up to Julie's house. They should be back shortly."

"Doesn't Julie live like an hour away?"

"About that, but she said it was important. Brent went with them. He wanted to check on the horses." Kaylee shook her head bemusedly. "They hired someone to look after the place and feed the animals for the weekend, but Brent is like a helicopter parent when it comes to his animals."

"Which reminds me," Paige said. "When is John arriving?"

"Tomorrow. He doesn't have a lot of vacation time, so he can only come up for Saturday and Sunday."

"This weekend is going to be a whirlwind, but think of all the precious memories your family is creating." Paige smiled. "I'm glad I get to be a part of it. Now, what can I help with?"

"James and Ben asked for pancakes," Kaylee said. "I already made the batter and am just waiting for the griddle to heat up."

Paige shuffled to the counter. "I'm on it, right after I pour myself some coffee."

Several dozen pancakes, two packages of bacon, and a carton of scrambled eggs later, she was finally able to pour herself a second cup.

"Good morning, beautiful." Warm breath caressed her cheek as Noah leaned in to whisper the greeting. His hair was sticking out on the left side of his head, while the right was plastered against his face. He looked adorable, and she liked his renewed openness. For the first time in years, he resembled the carefree boy she first met.

"Good morning, Noah." She liked how saying his name felt lovely on her tongue. "Pancakes, bacon, eggs, or cereal?"

"I'll start with coffee, and then go from there." He pulled the glass carafe off the coffee maker. "Have you had your breakfast yet?"

"No. I wanted to get the kids fed first."

He reached around her and took the spatula out of her hand. His body heat sent a warming sensation all the way down to her toes.

"Mmm, your hair smells like orange juice."

"Ella spilled her juice on me when James bumped her because Luke was trying to steal the last pancake." Paige chuckled, indicating she wasn't in the least bothered by the latest fracas.

"Oh, Lord." Julie entered the kitchen, back from the early morning trip with Mia and Brent and carrying a full brown paper bag, probably groceries. "I swear, he was not raised in this family."

"What?" He turned to mock-glare at his sister.

"You don't tell a woman she smells like orange juice. You tell her she smells irresistible, like the fragrance of orange blossoms or something romantic." Julie opened the refrigerator and started putting away the bag of groceries. "I'm going to have a talk with Brent and John, see if they can give you some pointers."

Paige couldn't help the rambunctious laughter hitting her all at once. She'd take any compliment Noah gave her, but Julie's interpretation was funny. She placed a hand on Noah's arm. "It's fine. Really. I like orange juice, but I think you might be smelling my honey and citrus conditioner."

"Maybe I'm adopted," he said, loud enough for Julie to hear.

"You were not adopted. You look just like dad." And he did. Same strong chin and quick smile and dark eyes under thick brows.

"Hey, Noah and Paige," Mia called from the living room. "Can you help me with something for a minute?"

"Sure. Let me wash my hands. They're a bit sticky." She pumped some soap onto her hands, scrubbed, and gave them a quick rinse before following Noah out of the kitchen into the other room, frowning at the solemn look on Mia's face.

Something was up. Julie and Kaylee were giving her assessing looks while Mia beckoned for them to follow her into one of the bedrooms, a pink garment bag over one arm.

"What's going on?" Paige asked, skin prickling with uneasiness.

Mia clasped her hands in front of her. "Noah and I were talking last night, and I realized there's a problem with my wedding."

Paige looked at Noah, but he didn't say anything.

"How can I help?"

"You can help by saying yes to the dress." Mia hooked the garment bag over the door and unzipped it, a cagey smile hovering on her face. "You see, I realized all my sisters are going to be in my wedding, but I missed one. You. Then I got to thinking. Julie ordered two bridesmaid dresses to see which one would fit better. This extra one might be a bit large, but with a little stitching, I'm sure you could make it fit."

"Is that where you went so early this morning?" Paige tried hard to ignore the sting in her eyes. "To get the dress so you could ask me to be in your wedding party?"

"You are my sister, are you not?"

"Well, technically, I'm Noah's sister-in-law, but—"

"No buts. I would really like it if you would be part of my wedding party. It would make the day complete." Mia reached for her hand. "Please say yes."

What was up with the Myers family? They were awfully hard to say no to.

She looked into Mia's determined face. "I would be so honored to be in your wedding."

Mia threw her arms around her and squeezed her tight. And in swept a calm surge of belonging. *She belonged*. She had finally found her beacon, a light to show her the way home. She pulled back. "I have a problem." A slice of panic pushed in.

Mia stepped back and the joy dimmed.

Paige felt a little naughty for spoiling the moment, but hoped Mia would forgive her. She pointed at the dress. "What am I going to do about shoes?"

Mia tipped her head back, her bliss returning. "Wear flip-flops if you want. The rest of us are wearing flats. The dress is floor-length, so no one will see."

Paige hugged Mia again. "Thank you." She glanced toward Noah, who mirrored what she was feeling. She was sure he had something to do with this, and she would thank him in private.

Mia gave her another quick squeeze before saying, "I'd better get going. I have a few details to go over before tomorrow. I'm getting married!" She squealed, waving her hands over her head as she danced out of the room.

Paige lifted the silvery sage material and stroked it. The color was soft and muted and would go perfectly with the purple and white flowers Mia had picked out.

She turned to Noah. "This was your idea, wasn't it?"

He moved in closer. "Actually, it was Mia's idea. I was telling her how hard funerals and weddings are for me, which led to her wondering if weddings are hard for you as well."

Paige remembered Olivia's wedding like it was yesterday. She'd spent the day getting her sister ready. The makeup was the worst part. Olivia's skin was so dry, her eyes had dark circles under them, and she had no eyebrows or lashes to speak of. And of course, the chemo had taken all the hair on her head, too. Olivia was so weak, just the ordeal of lying there to have her makeup done exhausted her. Paige spent the whole day fighting back tears. So yeah, the day had lacked typical wedding excitement, but she still felt blessed to have spent it with Olivia.

"Certain things in life are not comfortable, but we do them anyway because we need to. We grow up and move away from family to prove our independence. We have a difficult conversation with a colleague. We euthanize our sick animals. We live with regrets. But it's all part of life." Paige blinked away the swell of emotions. "I would not forfeit one moment I spent with my sister and when I watched you lift her in your arms to say her vows because she was too weak to stand. You made her happy. So, no. Weddings aren't hard. What's hard is saying goodbye."

Noah shoved his hands in his pockets and rocked back on his heels. "You were so strong that day. I remember you wore this blue number with sequins on the top."

Surprise made her gape at him. "I was supposed to wear that dress to the prom, but I never got to go. Olivia was too sick, so I decided to stay home to help. Besides, no one invited me to the prom."

"You missed out on a lot." Noah reached for her hand. "I know tomorrow is Mia's wedding, but what if we pretend it's your prom day? We'll dance. We'll drink champagne. It'll be perfect."

How could she say no to one of her unfulfilled bucket list items? She'd secretly fantasized about going to the prom with Noah. The reality of being his *for real* date for Mia's wedding wasn't something she'd ever imagined, but it gave her the courage to dream again. For so many years she'd struggled to accept that life wasn't fair, and it usually didn't turn out the way you wanted. Maybe this was fate telling her it was okay to hold on to those secret dreams, because sometimes they did come true.

"I'd love that, especially the champagne part. I love the way the bubbles tickle my nose."

"Then again, let's make another first. Paige Weaver, will you go to the prom with me?"

"A date and the prom." She waved a hand over her face and batted her eyelashes. "My, oh, my, Noah Myers, you sure know how to show a woman a good time." She rested a hand on his chest. "All kidding aside, it would be my honor." She did a little curtsy.

He took a bow. "Then, ma'am, it's a plan."

He leaned in and was inches away from kissing her when they heard little-girl giggles. They turned to see Emma peering around the door, her mouth bowed in a mischievous smile.

"Uncle Noah and Aunt Paige, sittin' in a tree…" She sing-songed the familiar childish taunt about K-I-S-S-I-N-G.

Disappointment washed over Paige.

Her whole being wanted to know what Noah's kiss would be like. Would he take his time? Would she feel it all the way down to her toes? Now she'd have to wait to find out because Noah had turned to shoo Emma out of the room and the moment was gone.

But she could wait.

This first kiss would be a precious memory to hold close to her heart when the wedding weekend was over and Noah returned to Singapore.

She let out a long sigh.

Maybe she should let Noah go. It would be the prudent thing for her heart.

She watched Noah sweep his niece into his arms and give her a raspberry kiss.

Who wouldn't love a man like Noah Myers?

Chapter 12

$\mathcal{E}$arly that afternoon, Noah watched Mia walk away across the resort's patio surrounding the pool, a band of tension circling his chest. He'd procrastinated about writing a wedding speech, but he was running out of time, as his sister just reminded him. He needed help, and knew just the person to tap for assistance.

He spotted Paige nearby, chatting with Emma while Paige kept an eye on the rest of the kids, who were splashing and screaming in the swimming pool. Paige wore an ankle-length dress with a light-blue floral pattern, fitting for an exclusive beach location with white sand, white-capped water, and emerald palm trees. He closed his eyes, imagining a soft breeze stirring the skirt of her dress and loose strands of hair across her shoulders as she waded into the languid waves.

She crouched low while Ella examined the bracelets adorning Paige's wrist. Several were made with colorful woven strings interlaced with beads, shells, and charms.

She stood up as he strode over to join them. "I was just telling Emma about my friendship bracelets. These were gifts from my students."

"Very nice." He squinted into the sun and did his best to set aside his agitation about the speech. "Um, Paige? I hate to bother you, but do you have a minute? I need to write a wedding speech and I don't know where to start. I figure you being an English teacher and all, you might…"

"You mean a toast?"

"Yeah, I guess. Mia said I have ten minutes. I can't even come up with something to fill thirty seconds."

Paige leaned down and whispered something in Emma's ear that sent her trotting off in the direction of Kaylee, who was also supervising the swimmers. "Let's go somewhere quiet. I'm sure between the two of us we can figure something out. Let's go over there."

At the far end of the pool, chairs and tables were set up for those who wanted to eat outside next to the flower garden. The place looked serene, but all he felt was a full-on panic.

Wedding toasts were supposed to highlight intimate details about the bride and groom, and he hadn't been around during their courtship. In fact, he could count on one hand the number of times he'd met Alec before the wedding. What was he supposed to say about a guy he didn't really know?

Paige settled at one of the tables in the shade and pulled a small notepad and pen out of her bag, looking at him expectantly.

"What? I don't have a clue where to start." He crossed a leg over his knee, pulling his calf closer while his free foot waggled with agitation.

"Look, this isn't difficult. You're overthinking it. The toast is nothing more than a heartfelt wish for the bride and groom's happiness with a few anecdotes thrown in for good measure. Think of something funny about Mia and some of the guys she's dated previously, and then how happy everyone in the family is that she ended up with Alec. Simple as that."

His jaw dropped as his anxiety thermometer fell below dread level. "You make it sound so easy."

She shrugged. "When people are given an assignment, whether it's Mia asking you to compose a toast for the wedding or my students tasked with completing an essay, it's easy to get overwhelmed, because you want it to be perfect and polished and error-free. You don't go from a blank page to the final version in one fell swoop. Let's start with a first draft."

"The challenge is, I don't know what to say." He dropped his foot to the ground and rested his elbows on his knees. "Over the past several days, I've been reminded how much I've missed, and no amount of time is going to give me those moments back."

Paige laid her pen on the table and studied his face. "So, what are you going to do about it? There's a saying: The best time to plan was ten years ago. The second-best time is now."

"All this time I believed I was doing the right thing by leaving. I was angry and didn't want my bad mood to rub off on my family." He pulled on his ear, with no idea what else to say. "Maybe I should have stayed and worked out my anger here."

Paige leaned closer and touched his hand. "Hey. Don't 'should all over yourself.' You made the best decision for yourself at the time. There's another old Chinese adage which says it's never too late to mend. You *are* here now. That's what counts."

"Is mending why you agreed to come back home?"

Paige looked past his shoulder toward the endless Pacific Ocean and the wide blue sky, her gaze focused on something far off in the distance. "I suppose it is. My mom and dad aren't getting any younger, and I don't want to live with regrets."

He got that. He had a ton of regrets, most of them centered around his family. "Sorry, I didn't mean to pry. Let's work on my speech. It's gotta be good."

"If you want it to be good, or even better, *great,* then you'll have to reach deep and open your heart, because that's where the best speeches come from."

"Yes, teacher." His worry had birthed a litter of new worries while they talked.

"It's not hard, Noah. Don't worry about the guests. Think about what you want to say to Mia and Alec. Do you remember your wedding toast?"

His gut tightened. "Olivia got tired before we even made it to the toast. We left while everyone else stayed for the dinner."

"Oh. Right. Maybe that wasn't a good idea. She's gone. We're here. Still living." Paige closed her eyes and dropped her hands into her lap.

"I know." And he did know. If he was going to be the person he wanted to be for his family, for Paige, he was going to have to change. Starting today. No more looking back. No more fear.

"Let's start again." Noah took a deep breath. "I want the speech to be funny. I used to be funny. I want to be that guy again. The one who makes people laugh. The one who rides cows, and the one who delivers flowers just to see people smile."

Paige nodded in favor of the idea. "Okay, let's start with funny. What would make Mia laugh, or writhe with embarrassment?"

He thought long and hard, and then a memory made his eyes light up. "In high school, I asked Mia to help me with a speech I was supposed to write. It sucked so bad, she had to write the whole thing. I think we should start there. I suck at writing speeches, which means I can write a really bad speech, but then give it a great twist at the end. What do you think?"

"I think that'll be a perfect start. From there you should find three standout experiences you and Mia had while growing up."

"You mean like the time she tried to stuff grapes up my nose, or the time she deflated my basketball and hid the air pump?"

Paige laughed, and he'd never seen anything so beautiful. Her checks turned rosy, and her eyes lit with joy. The wind caught the tendrils of her hair, and a long, curly strand blew across her face. She covered her mouth with her hand because she assumed she shouldn't be laughing, but her mirth reminded him life could be funny if the memory was twisted a little bit toward the positive.

That's what made Paige special.

Her ability to shine light toward the good.

"What about the day Mia convinced you she needed to practice her first aid skills to get a job as a lifeguard and she put you into a neck brace, secured you to a backboard, and then left you tied up?"

"I'd forgotten about that one." Noah chuckled. "That's a good one, especially since she's a doctor now."

The incident reminded him Paige had been there in the background, always watching, always waiting, always in the shadows. He didn't want her waiting in the wings anymore.

Noah reached for her hand. "Thank you." He leaned closer. "You've given me some great ideas."

She leaned closer, too, and he could smell her citrus shampoo, combined with her coconut sunscreen. The smell was soft, natural, and irresistible. He bent closer, drawn in by the sensual tip of her head. Wanting to feel her goodness seep into him.

"Noah! Paige!" He turned to see Julie hailing them from the pathway above the pool area. "It's time to get ready for the rehearsal dinner."

Rotten timing, sis.

Yes, the gang needed to get cleaned up for the wedding rehearsal and the casual dinner to follow, but he could have stayed there with Paige and never noticed time passing.

The thought of claiming Paige as his special someone within the circle of his family generated a kind of contentment he hadn't experienced in years. No, it was a sense of rightness, he realized, somewhat astonished by the thought.

"We'd better go." Paige slid her pen and notepad into her bag and stood, ready to jump in and help again.

This was supposed to be her vacation, and he intended to make sure she had time to relax.

"Oh, no." Paige moved closer to see his face. "What is that?" She made a swirling gesture with her finger around his face. "What are you worried about now?"

"You," he admitted. "I promised you a vacation, and here you are, being seamstress, cook, arts and crafts coordinator, and now speechwriter. Not a very relaxing break."

"Says who? You know I love kids. Besides, it's been a long time since I've been part of a family. It's fun watching everyone interact and hearing all the stories. The past few days have been just what I needed. It's made me realize how much I miss being connected. Since I move every few years to different jobs, I've been unable to build any deep connections. It's lonely sometimes."

She watched the group trudging back to the villa, Luke and James trying to snap Ben with their towels. Happy laughter rolled down the hillside. "I'm thrilled Mia asked me to be a part of her wedding. Just having her ask has made me feel like I haven't lost all connections."

He brushed a strand of hair off her face. "You have a special place in my heart. Always."

She searched his eyes and then stepped back, lifting her bag higher onto her shoulder, lips pressed in a thin line. "We should go. Everyone's waiting."

"Wait, Paige." He stopped her from walking away. "What just happened there?"

"Nothing happened."

"Something happened."

"Always?" She looked up at him, eyes dark with uncertainty. "That's what I'm worried about. I want always, but we aren't headed there. I'm your official date to the wedding, but then what?" Pain vibrated in her strained voice. "I don't see this turning into something permanent, and long-distance relationships are notoriously difficult. I…I won't deny I have feelings for you, Noah, but I'm having trouble with this…us…being temporary."

Fear sank in. He couldn't risk losing Paige, too. "It doesn't have to be." Noah shoved his hands in his pockets, unprepared for the pressure of defining feelings or expectations or relationship parameters, but unwilling to walk away.

She'd admitted she was in love with him, had been for ages, but what did that mean? Maybe it was just a schoolgirl crush matured into infatuation. What did real love—the kind that lasted forever—even feel like? He and Olivia had loved each other, but that love was the innocent, idealistic kind, that never had a chance to mature into something rich and seasoned. Now Paige was asking him to define the whirl of emotions he'd just discovered lurking in his heart.

"How can you say this isn't momentary when I'm staying here and you're going back to Singapore?"

"You could come with me," he suggested, surprised at how much he meant it. There was no fear or doubt. Her moving to Singapore was the perfect solution. "I'm sure you could find a job there. We'd have time to—"

"It was a big decision to move back here, and I'm finally ready to face the past instead of running from it." She shook her head. "And there's my mom to consider. She wasn't there for me when I needed her after Olivia died, but I never realized I left a gap when I took off, and she'd essentially lost both her girls. Family is important, Noah. You, more than anyone, should realize that."

He didn't know what to say.

He liked Paige—more than liked her.

But two or three days together, discovering mutual feelings, weren't sufficient justification for upending his life or asking her to do the same. He didn't know what the future held for them, so the right here and right now had to be enough.

"Don't worry. We'll think of something." He curved his arm around her waist, needing to touch her, connect with her, and thankful she didn't pull away.

Because, at whatever cost, he intended to keep Paige in his life.

Chapter 13

"*I* hope tomorrow's ceremony goes better than the rehearsal." Noah cupped Paige's elbow as they climbed the wooden steps from the wedding gardens near the resort's vineyards back to the main building. "Between the kids, the huge bridal party, and Alec's mother bursting into tears every five minutes, this is more like a three-ring circus than a wedding."

"It'll be perfect." Paige sighed. "This is a fairy-tale setting. I can see why Mia and Alec chose the resort for their venue. The rooms and villas make the event a vacation for guests, and the service has been impeccable. The gardens are beautiful, as are the sprawling vineyards, and, of course, the rocky coastline and the Pacific Ocean."

"Have you ever thought about what kind of wedding you want?" He deliberately slowed his pace, allowing the rest of the family and friends to pass them in the rush to dinner in the private dining room. Finding a quiet, separate moment with Paige during the past four hours had been impossible, and he was desperate enough to snatch any opportunity to explore the potential between them, even a few minutes walking from the gardens into dinner.

"I think every young woman fantasizes about her wedding, some more than others. One of the girls Mia and I went to high school with had every detail planned, from her dress to the music to the colors. But she hadn't even gone out on her first date yet." She laughed softly. "For me, it isn't so much the where, when, and how, as it was the who."

The image of Paige, dressed all in white, standing at the far end of an aisle, her eyes fixed on his, made his heart lurch. The ceremony with Olivia took place at the Weavers' home, and was limited to about thirty close friends and family because she was too sick for anything more formal. The limitations demanded by cancer was one of the main lures of working as a digital nomad. Nothing and no one tied him down. The problem was, he lacked any kind of grounding aside from the ties binding him to his family and Paige, who did more to anchor him than anyone else.

"I never wanted a big wedding," Paige went on. "But seeing everyone come together for Mia and Alec puts a different spin on things. It isn't about being the center of attention at a huge, fancy event, but surrounding yourself with the most important people in your life so you can all share a very special moment."

"Well said." Noah held the door for her to precede him into the main building.

They were the last to enter the noisy reception room, and everyone else was already seated or finding seats. Charley and Ben were supervising the other children at a long rectangular table set up off to one side. Julie and Brent's kids were responsible young adults and had willingly pitched in to help out when needed. Luke and James, Kaylee and John's boys, were more rambunctious, but they got along well with their sisters, Riley and Emma, and all of them adored baby

Max. Reece and Ethan, Logan's two, were close in age to Luke and James, but since arriving had clung to their dad. Watching Logan and his sons struggle with the aftermath of divorce broke Noah's heart.

This, right here, was a reminder that no one went through life unscathed. He'd had the luxury of running away from his problems, but that wasn't an option for Logan. Seeing what his brother and nephews were dealing with made Noah regret his earlier impatience with his older brother.

"Mia said it's open seating. Do you prefer something near the front or back?" Noah scanned the room from the doorway. "There are seats at the table with Aunt Rosa and my cousins, or that one in the corner where Mom and Alec's parents are sitting. I think Julie and Brent are headed that way."

"I like Aunt Rosa, but she'll probably try to pull us into a poker game." Paige threaded her arm through the crook of his elbow.

"How about drinks first, before the line at the bar gets too long?" He jerked his chin toward a setup at the far end of the room. "All this rehearsing has made me thirsty."

Noah admired the way Paige fit in, whether she was crouched at eye level chatting with his nieces and nephews or having a deep discussion about international politics with his brothers-in-law. She fit in, where others might have been intimidated by a raucous group of strangers.

She also had a knack for drawing people out through conversation and then remembering small details about them. One of the bridesmaids, a sorority sister from Mia's college days, was painfully shy. She hung back when the other bridesmaids practiced strolling down the aisle, some goofing around with silly dance moves. Paige had whispered something to the young woman that made her smile and relax. Whatever it was, it was still working, because the young woman was chatting and laughing with one of Alec's doctor friends, an attractive single guy just starting his pediatric oncology residency.

"You know, I always tend to think of us running off in separate parts of the world as a bad thing." He kept his voice low while they waited patiently to order glasses of wine. "After seeing how relaxed you are in a group like this and how adept you are at putting others at ease, I can't help but think there are some positive outcomes. You're confident, independent, fluent in foreign languages, and comfortable living and traveling to unfamiliar destinations and learning to navigate different cultures. Those aren't small accomplishments."

She didn't respond until they walked away from the bar, each holding a glass of the resort's vintage cabernet sauvignon.

"It's true there are lots of lessons to be learned."

"I like your positivity and unique approach to different situations." She took a small sip of the wine. "I don't have regrets about becoming a teacher and living overseas, but I want to come to terms with Olivia's death so I can move forward. You've reminded me of the importance of looking for the happy amid the sad, and focusing on the good, not just the bad."

Noah set his wine on the table so he could pull out Paige's chair. Once she was seated, he scooted her in and then lowered himself into the seat next to her. On his left sat Alec's father, a distinguished lawyer type, and next to him was his slim wife, who had tinted blond hair and a leathery tan testifying to many hours in the Arizona sunshine.

A quick round of introductions was made before Mia and Alec stood and wedding guests began tapping knives or forks against a nearby glass.

"We want to thank all of you for being a part of our wedding. We know each of you has invested time and money to be here with us, especially my brother Noah, who came all the way from Singapore, and Paige, who is like a sister to me, and who lives in Vietnam." Mia grinned as the group applauded.

"One of the best things about getting married is starting a new family. Not just me and Alec, but our parents, siblings, aunts, uncles, cousins, and friends who are like family." Mia wiped a tear away. "There is so much love in this room. Alec and I feel the support, but we want you to feel our embrace, too. That's the whole reason for a rehearsal dinner. Sure, the reception is flat-out bribery, especially when the food is prepared by an award-winning chef, but this is an opportunity for you to get acquainted with each other."

Mia opened her mouth to continue speaking, but Alec gently shushed her.

"My lovely wife-to-be would like to get philosophical at this moment, but I know you're hungry. Please enjoy the meal, have a second glass of wine as long as you aren't driving, and be sure to mix and mingle. The people gathered here are those we love the most, and we'll be seeing each other often in the future because…" Alec looked over at his parents with an encouraging nod.

His father stood up, glass raised, and shouted, "Family—first, last, and always."

Noah and the rest of the guests lifted their glasses and repeated the toast. It was true, Noah thought. They weren't losing a sister. They were expanding their family.

"I miss this." Paige had leaned close to whisper in his ear, her breath warm on his neck.

"Miss what?"

"Being a part of things. Having a place to belong. I have wonderful friends, but nothing compares to family."

His lungs locked up when he caught the expression on her face. "I'm super glad you came, Paige."

Pure love and happiness radiated from the sheen in her eyes and the smile curving her enticing mouth. And it was all directed at him.

"Thanks for convincing me to come. You were right, I would have regretted missing Mia's wedding. You and I already have too many regrets." She slid her hand onto his thigh under the tablecloth.

Noah made a vow to himself then and there. No more regrets. Paige had shown him a glimpse of what they could have together.

Now all that was left was finding a way to make the relationship work.

Something recent history had proven he wasn't good at. Maybe it was just a matter of making it work...with the right woman.

Chapter 14

*P*aige leaned back in her beach chair to watch the sun disappear below the horizon, crowned by orange and pink clouds. It was a beautiful ending to a beautiful day. Unfortunately, it also brought her one day closer to Noah's return to Singapore.

Sparks from the bonfire rose into the twilight sky like fireflies. The day had cooled enough so the heat from the flickering flames was welcome and inviting. She'd forgotten how much she enjoyed the sunny warmth of California summer days followed by cool nights perfect for bonfires, cozy sweatshirts, and cuddling close with someone special.

The resort attendant put another dried oak log on the pile in the firepit, causing a flurry of glowing embers to scatter upwards. She let her head fall back on the pillowed seatback and inhaled, filling her lungs with the smell of wood smoke, briny ocean, and earthy pine. The rugged California coastline was unlike anywhere else she'd traveled, and the familiar sights, scents, and sounds soothed her spirit.

She didn't know what to feel about Noah, but deep down she needed to let go of the past if she were to have any future. The rest of her life was essentially a blank canvas, and she was excited about creating something new and meaningful and fulfilling.

Facing the past wouldn't be easy, finding a new job would be a challenge, and redefining her relationship with her parents would take time, but Paige wasn't afraid anymore. She'd proven she was strong and resourceful and resilient. It was time to stop running from life and confront it head-on.

"You look like you're deep in thought." Noah's husky voice pulled her back to the present.

He sat on the other side of a small round table set between the chairs for glasses and small plates. She lifted her glass of wine, sniffing appreciatively at the rich cherry and intense currant character of the sweet, dark burgundy drink.

"Just enjoying all this. I forgot how much I love the California coastline."

"And I thought the outstanding company put that smile on your face." He raised his own wineglass in a sardonic salute.

Other guests gathered around firepits along the beach, a guitarist in the near distance serenading them with classic folk songs from James Taylor, Bob Dylan, Paul Simon, and Harry Chapin. She and Olivia grew up listening to those songs, the music of their parents' generation. The simple melodies and poetic lyrics filled Paige with a longing to go back in time for a chance to do things differently. For a chance to stay instead of running. To hold onto the connection with her parents instead of allowing her relationship with them to fall apart. To reach out to Noah, not as a friend or a sister-in-law, but as a woman in love.

"Nothing like red wine and James Taylor to make you sentimental." He drained the last bit of ruby-red liquid from his glass. "I turn forty this year, and I can't help but think I'm halfway through my life. Where did the time go? Once upon a time I had my whole life mapped out."

She was feeling the same way, but she had the advantage being six years younger. Then the thought occurred to her: did the age gap make much of a difference now that they were older? Her feelings were unchanged, maybe more mature. Noah mesmerized her. She could watch him all day long. The way he talked with his hands. The way his mood showed on his face. The way he always wanted to be in the one place he could help the most.

"Which begs the question," she nudged his bare foot with the toe of her sandal, "what *are* you going to do with the rest of your life?"

"I don't know." He laced his hands behind his head and gazed out to the ocean. "Before Olivia got sick again, we had all kinds of plans. Stuff we wanted to do together and on our own, and forty seemed such a long way off. I figured by now I'd have a couple of kids, a job at a Silicon Valley tech company, and a house in the suburbs. After Olivia died, those plans went out the window. It felt selfish to do all the things we'd talked about doing together without her, and I didn't have a backup plan."

"Why can't you still have those things?"

"My adolescent brain believed that without Olivia those things weren't important anymore." He looked around the group at his mother, smiling proudly at Mia and Alec, who were holding hands, and the rest of his siblings and their partners. "Priorities change when there are two people's needs to consider. It's just been me for sixteen years."

"That's a long time to be alone," she said, an echo of her own lonely stretch adding intensity to her comment.

"I'm surprised you aren't married with a six-pack of kids. I thought most women's biological clocks started ticking away by thirty." He shared a meaningful look.

"You're so good with kids. Seeing you with this bunch makes me appreciate what a dedicated teacher you must be."

"Not everyone chooses to have children." She couldn't help the defensive edge in her tone.

"It's the cancer thing, isn't it? You don't want to worry about passing on the genes." He seemed unfazed by her bristly attitude.

"Something like that." She bit her lip, afraid Noah would be horrified to know the truth.

How could she explain? She didn't want to go through what her parents had endured? Watching a six-year-old go through chemo, taking a child to doctor appointments and hospital stays instead of dance lessons and birthday parties? Olivia wasn't the only one who missed out on a normal childhood. As much as her parents tried to maintain a normal home environment, everything centered around Olivia. Long, dark days when she was sick; hectic, happy days when she was well.

"I never stopped to imagine what growing up with a deathly ill older sister must have been like for you." In the glow of the firelight, Noah's dark eyes glimmered with compassion.

"The cancer overshadowed every aspect of our lives. Her condition dictated what we could or couldn't do. Her treatments dominated our schedule. Paying for prescriptions and copays and home care ate up our finances. Sometimes I resented Olivia for being sick, even though I knew it wasn't her fault."

Like so many times before, Noah understood without her having to elaborate or make excuses.

"I remember screaming at my mom, asking her why I couldn't have a normal life." Paige rubbed the goose bumps on her arms. "She said I would never be like everyone else because I wasn't living an ordinary life. I wanted a better answer, but there wasn't one to be found."

"I know your childhood was difficult." The ferocity in Noah's gaze caused everything else to fade away. "Some people would have been crushed by the experience, turned bitter and angry. But your mom was right; you're far from ordinary. In fact, you're quite extraordinary. Look at all the lives you've touched and influenced, like that Vietnamese boy and his mother."

Noah grabbed her hand and started playing with her fingers while a wave of tingles ran up her arms. But part of her wondered whether this was real, or if he was just caught up in the wedding festivities. The problem was, she'd seen him fall hard for a woman before, only to find the new love interest lacking in some way just weeks later.

"Do you mind if I ask you a question?" She stared into the flames.

"No. Shoot."

"Let's pretend this weekend is over. We've had a great time at the wedding. You've finished your website design—which you still need to do, by the way—and it's time for you to return to Singapore while I remain in California. What happens then?"

Noah pulled back his hand and looked away without saying a word.

The realization she'd been right hit her. Noah didn't do long term. Not anymore. And she refused to be his short-term fix.

The agony of facing the fact stole her breath and triggered a fiery pain in her chest.

She pushed out of the chair. "Right. I think I'll go for a walk." She turned to wave Noah off. "Don't get up. Enjoy your time with your family."

She took a deep breath and headed for the wooden plank

stairs leading to the garden path, grateful for an opportunity to be alone with her thoughts without having to hide them.

As she walked, her life rewound, and she hit the replay button, pausing a moment at each pivotal influence that had shaped her life. Idolizing Noah, worshipping her beautiful older sister, watching Olivia die, losing her parents to divorce, leaving California, getting her teaching certificate, and skipping around through Poland, Costa Rica, Thailand, and then Vietnam.

Maybe the most significant event was her own cancer diagnosis. She'd been too afraid to tell anyone, even her own parents, and handled it all on her own in a foreign country, far from home. Dealing with the Big C without a support system was really hard, but she couldn't burden anyone else —anyone who might panic over her possible mortality.

She felt so alone and longed for a close connection.

Sixteen years of not having a close connection had sucked her dry, and she wondered whether her willingness to be with Noah was a desperate attempt to hold off the spiral of loneliness.

She sighed as she reached the villa door.

The place was quiet, the kids already in bed. It had been a long day for everyone, and the fatigue weighed her down, along with the troubling, unanswered questions. She thought she'd left everyone on the beach, but a solitary figure at the kitchen table proved her wrong.

"Hey, there." Mrs. Myers smiled and patted the table. "I have water on for tea if you'd like a cup of chamomile before bed."

The lure of a sympathetic maternal ear was irresistible. Paige sat down and watched the older woman prepare two cups of tea.

Returning to the table, Mrs. Myers said, "Tell me, what did my son do now? Having been raised in a family of ten, raising five of my own, and having nine grandchildren, I'm a pretty good judge of people. Especially when it comes to reading hurt or disappointment. And you, missy, walked in the door looking like someone had just killed your pet rabbit." Mrs. Myers reached for her hand. "Talk to me, Paige. I'm a good listener."

Oh, no. The sting behind her eyes started again, then her nose began to run, and giant streams of tears rolled down her face. A box of tissues appeared in front of her while the tea cooled. As hard as Paige tried, she couldn't stop the tears. A torrent still streamed down her face.

"I'm sorry." She again willed the hurt to stop.

"For what, child?"

"Have you ever wanted something so much you waited and waited and waited for it, and just when it was finally right there in front of you, you were afraid to reach out and grab it for fear it wasn't real?"

"You're talking about Noah."

She nodded, dabbing at her damp eyes. "Sometimes I wish my sister was still here. There are a few choice words I'd like to say to her."

"Like what?"

"Like why did it have to be her, not me? She was the smart one, the pretty one, the one everyone loved."

"The one Noah loved." Mrs. Myers spoke so quietly Paige almost didn't hear her.

She raised her eyes to look into the soft, lined face. "I tried so hard not to be a burden, to be invisible so my parents didn't have to worry, but I got so good at standing in the background, the one person I most wanted to notice me still can't see me."

"Oh, he sees you, Paige. He sees you and knows you better than anyone else, but he's afraid of what he feels for you." She came around to Paige's chair and bent to wrap an arm across her shoulders, embracing her in a comforting hug and smelling of Ivory soap and wood smoke. "He'll come around. He will. You just need to be patient a little longer."

"I'm not so sure." Her sniffle sounded pathetic and wimpy.

Mrs. Myers ran a hand down her hair. "Is this the first time you've cried?"

She leaned back and looked up into the woman's wise countenance. The soft creases around her eyes made Paige accept the deep wisdom in the woman's gaze. "How did you know?"

"Just a feeling. I know something to help you feel better." Mrs. Myers waddled over to the portable crib in the corner of the room and lifted out the sleeping Max. She cradled him in her arms and brought him to Paige, adjusting the baby blanket while Max stretched his arm.

Paige let his tiny fingers wrap around her index finger. "He's still asleep."

"There is one thing about life we must all learn. Every life begins and ends. What matters is what we do with the in-between. If you're afraid to live or afraid to die, then there lies the problem. Because not living is the same as dying, and both you and Noah are stuck. There are no two people on this planet who need each other more than you two. I just hope you both reach an understanding before you waste too much more time."

The front door opened and closed, and footsteps rushed in. The way Mrs. Myers patted her cheek and reached out for the baby revealed who had walked through the door.

Noah walked around the edge of the table, sharp eyes examining her face, a frown marring his handsome face.

"You've been crying." Noah reached for her hand. "I've been searching everywhere for you. After you left, I replayed the conversation and realized I'd been a jerk. Again. Listen, Paige—"

"You don't have to explain."

"No, I do. You see, I think I want this to work between us so badly, I'm afraid to say the wrong thing. And not saying anything is also making me screw up."

Wow. She didn't see this coming. "You want this—us?—to work?"

He nodded and his grip on her hand tightened. "Yeah, I do. I don't have all the answers right now, but you're here and I'm here. We're adults. I keep thinking we should be able to figure this out, but…I don't know. It just seems like things keep getting in the way."

Paige collected her used tissues, and wadded them up in the palm of her hand, not wanting Noah to notice the evidence of her tears and misery.

He sat down in the chair his mother had vacated. "Would you stay for a few days after the wedding? That would give me time to finish my project, and then we could go down to LA and visit your mom, or wherever else you would like to go. I don't care what we do, as long as we're together. How does that sound?"

"That sounds great." Happiness replaced the hopelessness in her heart.

"Yeah?" His concern turned into excitement.

"It will be nice to spend time together." She turned her hands so theirs were palm-to-palm. "But why do we have to wait until after the wedding?"

His smile started slow and then lit up, like a flame setting a piece of timber on fire. He reached for the courage she knew to be somewhere inside. "It's a nice evening. Maybe we can take a walk. The moon is full. And suddenly I'm not tired anymore."

There was nothing on earth more stunning than Noah's

crooked smile. She'd been there the day he was popped in the mouth playing football, and again when Logan broke his nose during a game of frisbee.

She'd been there for the living part. But she couldn't bear to be there after the fear locked his heart and threw away the key.

"Or would you rather sit here and eat ice cream?" She tilted her chin toward the freezer. "I'm sure there's plenty left."

"Can't we do both?"

"Absolutely." He held out his hand, and she slid her fingers into his.

Chapter 15

"I can't remember the last time I ate so much ice cream." Paige paused to lick the melted butter pecan drippings off her spoon.

Noah's gut tightened, but he kept pace with Paige while they ambled along the white sandy beach, the almost-full moon lighting their way.

There was nothing overtly sensual in her pleasure, but Noah's abs tightened with longing. Admitting he had feelings for her had opened the door, loosing a cascade of emotions, desires, hopes, and dreams that he'd never allowed to see the light of day.

Each moment, each new shared experience, each facet she revealed, made Noah want to stop and cradle the discovery so he could examine and admire its nuances before adding it to the new collection—one to be appreciated every day.

She transformed simple, everyday actions into moments and memories too precious for words. Every detail of this moment—their first moonlight walk—was being permanently etched into his soul like the scenes and phrases chiseled onto stone by the ancient Egyptians, Greeks, and Romans.

"The last time was probably when you were around my family. There's always plenty of ice cream to go around. Open any freezer and you'll find at least three cartons in different flavors." He dug another large scoop of rich, creamy strawberry out of the cereal bowl, adding to the sweetness of the moment.

"Ice cream allows us to tap into our inner child." Paige gave his hand an affectionate squeeze. "It's sugary, creamy, and gooey. Kids love to touch, feel, taste, even make a mess. It's how they learn."

"Making messes is also how they drive their parents crazy," he teased. "Ask Kaylee about the time John took a break while he was painting Emma's bedroom to chat with his boss on the phone. Ten minutes was plenty of time for Luke and James to get into the open cans of paint and *help*." He laughed, remembering the pictures Kaylee sent him. "There were dribbles of princess pink paint trailed down the hall, splattered on the stairway banister, and all over the boys' faces and clothes."

Paige chuckled while they meandered farther down the beach, the bonfires and noise far behind them. She took a bite of the flaky, sugary wafer stuck in the middle of the ice cream mound, the crunch loud over the whisper of waves caressing the hard-packed sand.

The temptation to lean in and lick the sugary taste off Paige's lips was making Noah's mouth water.

"Your mom sure is dropping hints about wanting more grandkids. Do you ever regret not having kids?" she asked, her voice tentative.

His sensual thoughts evaporated while he considered her question.

Funny how a month ago, maybe even a week ago, that

question would have angered him. The decision to have children—or not—was one of the many choices taken from him when Olivia died. For years he only remembered what he lost, the events beyond his control, the hopes and dreams that would never be realized.

Paige, with her kindness and compassion and unconditional acceptance, put things into perspective. Gave him a different, softer, more optimistic perspective. He was still adjusting to this shift, but Paige's nonjudgmental question enabled him to reach beyond the anger or resentment and get to the core of his thoughts.

"Sometimes I feel like the only things I have to show for all my time on earth are regrets and wishes for different outcomes." He dropped the spoon into his ice cream bowl. "If only Olivia had recovered. If only I had stayed in California. If only I went to college with my buddies. Regrets come with the assumption that if only, then…then my life would be perfect, then I'd never experience grief, then I'd have everything I want."

He turned to the beautiful woman at his side. "You've shown me that I still have choices. I want to live in the moment and allow amazing things to come into my life instead of holding onto the past and all those regrets."

"You've summed up exactly what I've been thinking, Noah." Paige sniffled and turned to him with a seriousness he hadn't seen before. "But you didn't answer my question."

The bowl in his hand rocked, slopping the rich contents over the side to spill over his knuckles and fingers.

He snorted a laugh. It was just like her to call him out. "It's natural to regret things we miss out on, but we can't know how those choices would have turned out."

He stopped to link his sticky fingers with hers, then lifted their hands for a quick lick of ice cream and butter pecan. "There are benefits to being an uncle. I get all the fun with none of the responsibility." He held up his ice cream bowl. "All the creamy, yummy, messy fun."

Paige threw back her head and laughed, the crystalline notes of happiness floating up toward the stars. Her joy was one of the most beautiful things he'd ever seen.

"Sorry," she choked out, wiping tears off her cheeks. "I left the wet wipes on the counter."

"Let's head back. The kids might have fun making a mess, but I can't wait to get rid of this sticky stuff and wash my hands."

They strolled back toward the resort, hands swinging between them. A brief pang of guilt needled Noah, but then faded when a sense of rightness filled him. Second-guessing life, his decisions, even himself, had become a habit, but deep down in his heart he knew he was exactly where he was.

"Have you ever been carefree?" Paige nodded toward a rowdy group of young adults singing around a bonfire.

The group of six had separated into couples, with their arms slung around each other in a circle, rocking in unison while they sang loudly, accompanied by a fellow strumming a guitar. The song ended, and a couple of the guys raised bottles of beer in a salute of sorts while loud applause filled the night.

"Not for a long time." He dropped her hand so he could curl his arm around her waist, pulling her tight against his side. "After what we've been through, it's hard to hold on to that innocence."

Noah kept his arm around her waist while they continued strolling down the beach.

"I always thought it would be awkward to walk glued to someone's side, but this is nice." Paige lowered her voice so only he could hear her now that other people were nearby. "We seem to be a perfect fit."

"I enjoy having you close." A rush of desire heated his

skin, the cool night air a sensual contrast. He'd wanted other women since Olivia and had been intimate with a handful of his more serious girlfriends, but this yearning was so much more than lust.

He wanted to see and touch every inch of Paige's silky skin. Hear her breath hitch when he brushed his lips along her collarbone, between her breasts, and over her belly. Savor the taste of her kisses. Worship and honor her. Prove to himself this was real and lasting.

He fled California to avoid dealing with the pain of losing Olivia, and a remnant of that fear still fluttered in the back of his mind, but Noah was determined to stop running and figure out how to move forward.

If Paige could dig deep for the courage to reveal that she cared for him, she deserved a man who was willing to do the same.

When they reached the narrow path to the resort, he spotted the family villa ahead. The windows were dark, with only the path footlights and porch light to guide them.

When they reached the villa, Noah opened the door, stacked Paige's bowl on top of his half-empty one, and placed them in the sink before washing the goo off his hands while Paige waited at the end of the hall.

Then they tiptoed into their bedroom, shushing each other like middle-schoolers sneaking home after missing curfew.

He flipped on the bathroom light so he could see Paige, leaving the rest of the bedroom draped in shadow.

"This is so confusing." He settled his hands on her hips and looked down into her face. "You're still Paige, the same woman I've known for years, but the context is different. You're not Paige, my sister-in-law. You're Paige"—his fingers tightened, and he drew her flush against his hips—"the woman I want to kiss."

The inside of his eyelids burned, and a knot of emotion tightened his throat.

"May I kiss you good night?" His voice was ragged.

Paige blinked—once, twice—her long lashes fluttering against her cheeks. She cupped his face in her hands, raised up on her toes, and pressed her mouth against his.

Their first kiss was soft, reverent, then progressed into teasing and tasting, and elevated into hungry and demanding. Noah lost track of time, and he backed Paige up until he could lower to her bunk. He lifted himself over her body to lie next to the wall and pulled her into his arms.

The hurried kisses slowed, becoming more soulful—two people communicating needs and hopes without uttering a word. Each scent and sound and sensation embedded Paige deeper into his heart.

The long day closed in around them, and she curled up like a kitten, her head on his shoulder, her breath and movements slowing until she fell asleep.

Right then and there, Noah vowed he was done with regrets.

Chapter 16

*N*oah stood next to Logan and the other groomsmen while Mia and Alec exchanged vows, but his attention kept wandering back to Paige.

She looked like a beautiful piece of sea glass washed ashore, her beauty standing out among all the ordinary pebbles. She'd done her hair up into an elaborate twist and let her natural curls fall about her face and neck, and the soft, silvery-green fabric of the off-the-shoulder dress showed off her tanned skin.

He wished he was close enough to savor her natural scent again.

She looked like a goddess of femininity, and breathtakingly gorgeous. She seemed like an organic extension of the elegant setting for the ceremony, which was a beautifully landscaped garden created especially for weddings and similar ceremonies, with the resort's vineyards on one side and the ocean and forested cliffs on the other.

His hands curled into loose fists with impatience to touch her again and share another passionate kiss like the one shared on the villa doorstep, away from prying eyes.

Vigorous clapping forced him to focus on Alec once again, who was kissing his sister, bending her slightly backward as she held on.

He would have liked to do the same to Paige.

Mia and Alec turned and waved at everyone before walking back along the white carpet runner while the crowd tossed birdseed into the air around them. When they reached the garden archway steps leading up to the main lodge, they waited for the rest of the wedding party.

Noah reached the steps just behind Kaylee and John, and waited for Paige to catch up.

"The photographer needs everyone to head to the beach." Mia swooped her arms toward the stairs to the right like she was trying to herd ducklings instead of people. "Family photos. Everyone. Let's go. Chop, chop!"

Paige climbed the stairs holding Emma's hand. His niece seemed to have taken to her like kids to candy. And from the look on Paige's face, the feelings were mutual.

"The photographer wants the family down on the beach to take pictures. And that includes you." He took Emma's other hand while, a wistful look crossed Paige's face and then vanished.

"The kids are going to be a handful. I'll keep them occupied while the main pictures of the family are taken, or until they're needed." She lifted Emma into her arms and cuddled his niece, who was adorable in her dusky lavender tulle dress with lace at the hem. The two of them together looked like a photographer's dream come true.

Paige paused at the bottom step to help Emma take off her shoes, and as soon as the little girl managed to unbuckle her flats, she took off after her older brothers.

"Have I mentioned you look beautiful today?"

"Three times, actually." Paige glanced up as she retrieved

Emma's shoes, pink tinting her cheeks. "But I like hearing you say so. You don't look so bad yourself. I like the matching sage vest and bow tie. You look mighty handsome, Mr. Myers."

"I wish I wasn't committed to a minute-by-minute wedding agenda for the next several hours. I'd like to find a nice quiet place and show you just how beautiful you are."

"Noah!" Julie waved at him from the group gathering near the surf line.

"You'd better go. I'll round up the kids." She patted his cheek, trailing her fingers along his jaw.

Noah trudged through the sand toward the large gathering of family, but his eyes never strayed far from her.

The photographer staged the first series of pictures, and then called for the wedding party to come together, first for the groom, then the bride. Noah's irritation began to spike when Mia insisted on a picture of the groomsmen by themselves, with the bride, without the bride, with the bridesmaids, and the list went on and on and on. Even Alec mumbled something about needing a beer.

Noah pulled at his collar, trying to loosen his bow tie.

"Family photo," the photographer called.

Noah stood next to Logan and looked around. Paige pointed the kids toward the group so they could be included, but she held back.

She was so beautiful, with her skirt and curly tendrils blowing slightly in the breeze.

He squinted into the sunlight as the photographer was about to snap the shot, but it dawned on him not everyone was in the picture.

"Olivia. Come on." Noah raised his arm and waved. "It's the family portrait. You need to be in this shot."

The chittering of the entire group faltered like everyone had suddenly slammed into a wall going sixty miles an hour.

Logan turned, glared, and looked like he was about to break Noah's nose.

"That's okay," Paige yelled back. "Go ahead. I just need to run to the restroom."

Mia fell out of line, picked up her skirts, and stomped across the sand until she was about stepping on his toes. "What's wrong with you?"

"What?" He looked at his mother and Julie who had similar expressions.

"You don't even know, do you?" Mia poked at his chest.

"Ow." He shrugged away. "Why is everyone giving me dirty looks?"

"Because you just called Paige by her sister's name, you idiot. You called her Olivia." Logan glared at him, his jaw clenched. "You screwed up royally this time."

His mom shuffled over, her long sleeves flapping in the wind. "Okay, okay, everyone. Calm down. This can all be resolved after they've finished taking photos. Let's all just smile for the camera and then you," his mom pointed at him, "will find Paige and apologize."

"The rest of the wedding pictures are going to be ruined now," Mia smacked him on the arm, "You're such a jerk."

No one knew that better than he did. "I'll go find Paige and apologize now."

"No." Logan's tone held a warning. "You are going to stand next to me and smile as if nothing happened, because Mia and Alec deserve to have nice memories of this day."

After each shot, Noah searched the pathway back to the resort. There was no sign of Paige. It killed him that he'd hurt her. Again.

"Let's do another family shot," Mia suggested

"Oh, come on," Noah groaned.

"The reception is starting right after the photo shoot, so just cool your jets," Logan reminded him. "You need to be there for the reception line to greet the guests. For this one, bro, you don't get to be absent."

"What does that mean?" he asked, his voice tight. It was a warning for his brother to lay off since Noah knew what Logan was hinting at. Over the past sixteen years, he'd missed a lot of important events. His dad's funeral, his nieces' and nephews' births, birthdays, anniversaries, and the small but significant milestones in each person's life.

Guilt gathered beneath the sore spot where Mia had poked him.

"What am I supposed to do about Paige? She's obviously upset." He clamped his hand on his brother's shoulder as directed by the photographer, fingers gripping harder than necessary.

"You'll just have to talk to her when there's a break." Logan forced a smile for the camera.

Logan didn't look any happier than Noah felt, and it dawned on Noah the wedding reminded his brother of his own marital failure. He lightened his grip on Logan. "Seems like the Myers menfolk are always wishing for a do-over."

Logan glanced over his shoulder, sharing a moment of understanding. "Relationships are complicated, man. I hope you two get it right."

Noah again scanned the pathway, hoping to see Paige returning to the beach. But she still wasn't back after countless more photos. When the picture-taking finally finished, he broke from the group and started toward the steps, but his mother's voice stopped him mid-stride.

He waited, his hands shoved in his pockets while she made her way to him.

Even at five-foot-two, his mother looked intimidating. "What are you going to do, Noah? What are you going to say to Paige, hmmm?"

He looked up the stairway while not one idea came to mind.

"I messed up, Mom." Regret coiled with frustration. It wasn't like he committed the act intentionally. It was an honest mistake.

"Yes, you did, but if you go stalking after her like a lion, you just might get bitten. She's wounded." She laid a hand on his arm. "Give her a few more minutes to calm her hurt. Then she'll be able to hear what you have to say."

"I don't know, Mom." His gut churned with indecision. "I keep messing up."

"Oh, Noah. You need to be kinder to yourself. None of us are perfect. I know you want to make everyone happy, and you don't like conflict. Not even you can make everyone laugh all the time. You need to give yourself a break." She patted him on the cheek. "I know you're a good man. I just wish you knew it as well."

"It might help if everyone didn't keep reminding me I'm a jerk and what an awful brother and uncle I've been. I think they forgot I send cards every birthday and holiday, and make sure to get the kids what they have on their wish lists."

"You haven't heard what they're saying, Noah. Your brother and sisters are each telling you in their own way that they miss you. The real Noah. The one they grew up with. The funny, carefree boy. Not the one who gave up his dreams to marry a young woman dying of cancer and then ran away because he couldn't save her."

"Is that what you think happened?"

"Isn't it?" His mother's eyes narrowed as she challenged him to deny the truth.

And it was the truth.

He'd done everything to try to save Olivia. He prepared healthy meals, made sure she took her medication, scoured the internet for clinical trials, accompanied her to all her medical appointments. He did everything in his power to make sure she survived, but in the end he failed.

In his mind, he understood that if the doctors couldn't save her, he didn't stand a chance. But in his heart he felt like a failure. At least the twenty-three-year-old him believed he was a failure. The forty-year-old didn't know what to believe anymore.

"Fine. Olivia died, and I left." He paced away then back. "You know I couldn't stay here."

"I do know. It broke my heart to see you go. You will always be my baby, but I understood. Your siblings, not so much. Keep in mind that, to Julie and Kaylee, you were their child as well. When I was busy working, they took care of you. It also hurt them to see you go. Mia? Well, she was lost without you. And Logan, he was just mad. You left him to fend off all his sisters by himself." His mother's smile helped, but it wasn't enough to make him feel better. "Are you too old for your mother to give you a hug?"

"Heck, no." He wrapped his arms around her, resting his chin on top of her head. "I love you, Mom."

"I love you, too, Noah. So do your sisters and brother. They would do anything for you. All you have to do is ask."

"Do you think Mia would let me skip the reception?"

His mother pointed a finger at him. "Mia might, but I won't." She walked with him up the steps toward the main building where the reception was being held. "But as soon as Paige returns, I will make sure you have a moment in private. Knowing Paige, she's already forgiven you."

"I don't know about that." Noah held onto his skepticism.

"She's a lovely woman, that Paige. You'll see, everything will be okay."

He hoped his mother was right because Noah just had an epiphany.

No matter what, he couldn't live without Paige in his life.

Chapter 17

*P*aige lifted her skirt and sprinted up the stairs while she fought back the burning hurt. She wasn't going to cry. She never cried. She didn't cry when Olivia died, and she didn't cry when the doctor told her she had cancer.

She only cried when it came to Noah.

Again, he'd hurt the ten-year-old girl who fell so hard for her older sister's boyfriend. As an adult, she finally admitted to herself that she had no chance with Noah. None.

She couldn't bear to see him again.

Noah would explain away the gaffe as a slip of the tongue, but Paige knew better. There had been too many times over the weekend when Olivia was the first thing he mentioned during a conversation. Clearly she was still first and foremost on his mind…which also meant front and center in his heart.

She yanked open the door and raced to the resort's reception area, thankful there wasn't a line at the concierge desk.

"Can you please tell me when the next airport shuttle will be leaving?"

A perky young brunette woman pulled a clipboard from beneath the counter. "Are you looking to go to San Francisco or Oakland?"

"Oakland would be preferred, but I'll take either." Paige's heart pounded while she waited, noting the concierge name was Amy.

"Oakland leaves in twenty minutes."

Paige calculated the time it would take to pack. There was no other choice. She'd have to make the timing work. "I'll take it. My name's Paige. Paige Weaver. I have five suitcases. Can the shuttle pick me up in front of the Myers villa?"

"Certainly. Ms. Weaver. It would be our pleasure."

"Oh, and one more thing. Would you be able to help me find a flight to LA tonight?"

Amy kept her pleasant smile in place even as she took note of Paige's agitation, the slight lift to her eyebrows revealing her awareness.

"Certainly. Do you have any seat preference?"

"Any seat will do. I'll do standby if I must."

"I bet I can find you something. Oh! A shuttle cart just pulled up to the front door, so the driver can take you up to your villa now." Amy leaned closer. "And if you're a few minutes late, it'll be okay. There's only one other passenger, and you should make it to the airport in plenty of time. I'll be sure to give your flight confirmation to the driver once I've found something. The cost should be less than three-hundred dollars. Would it be okay to charge the card on your account if that's the case?"

"Yes. Thank you for your help, Amy. I appreciate it. May I borrow a pen and a piece of stationery?"

"Certainly."

With shaky fingers, Paige scribbled her note and folded

the piece of paper, then handed the pen and paper back. "Would you make sure Noah Myers gets this note? He's with the wedding party."

"Absolutely."

Paige closed her eyes. Amy's kindness had unhinged her control, and she was fighting not to lose it right then and there. "Thanks, Amy. I appreciate your help. I'd better go. I need to make that shuttle."

"Good luck," Amy called after her.

Paige's mind was already on getting to the villa and packing. As she climbed into the golf cart, she made a mental list of where all her belongings were stored. It shouldn't take her long to pack, since she made certain to remove her makeup bag and toiletries from the bathroom every morning. Before she could get all the way through her checklist, she arrived at the villa and was unzipping her borrowed dress as she raced through the kitchen.

It took only a few minutes to pull on some sweatpants and a T-shirt and toss everything else into her carryon. She dragged her luggage and backpack to the door, heaving a sigh of relief after the last bulky suitcase. A knock sounded, and she opened up to let the driver take her bags as she dashed back to the bedroom to make sure she had packed everything.

She ran her eyes over the silver sage fabric of the bridesmaid gown on a hanger hooked over the closet door. "I'm sorry, Mia. You were such a beautiful bride today." She hurried to the kitchen and pulled off a sheet of paper towel, grabbed a pen, and wrote, "For Emma," and removed her favorite bracelet, leaving both on the counter.

As she walked back to the front door, she memorized the little things identifying a family-occupied the villa. The baby crib, the shoes and socks on the floor, the coloring books, the stack of computer tablets—all the clutter she'd never be able to cherish. She closed the door.

"Are you ready, miss?" the driver asked while he handed her a ticket for her stored luggage and a thick white envelope with the resort's logo on the front. "Amy says your flight is all booked, and we should arrive at the airport in plenty of time for you to make the connection."

She could only nod as she removed her phone from her backpack and boarded the shuttle bus, taking a seat in the far back.

She watched out the window while the shuttle made its way from the parking lot and headed toward the coastal highway.

She pulled out her phone and dialed.

"Paige?" Her mom's voice held a note of surprise.

"Hey, Mom." She fought back her emotions. "I need a favor."

"Of course, honey. Is everything okay?"

No. Everything wasn't okay. Not even close.

"I'm sorry this is last minute, but I'm catching a flight down to LA tonight. Can I stay with you until I figure things out?"

"Yes. I'll pick you up if you tell me what time your flight arrives. I was already looking forward to our visit." Her mom's tone shifted and became tentative. "You sound upset. I hope it's not about coming home. I know I haven't always been there for you. But I want you to know I'm here for you now. I've never told you how sorry I am for being an absent mom to you all those years…you know…before."

Paige pushed up straighter in her seat and her jaw dropped. She gripped her phone tighter and closed her eyes. "You did the best you could." Her gut sent out a warning. "Mom, is everything all right? Your cancer's not back, is it?"

"No, honey. My breast cancer hasn't returned. I'm just

getting older and facing my regrets. You will too when you get to be my age. And my relationship with you is at the top of the list. I've wanted to fix what's broken, but I don't know how to start. Will you help me?"

"I have regrets of my own, Mom. And I would like for us both to mend the past. That's why I'm coming home instead of taking another foreign assignment. At least, not right away. If I can, I'd like to find an online job and perhaps work toward completing my college degree, maybe even pursue a master's."

Both would keep her busy, too busy to think about Noah. If Noah couldn't be a part of her life, she'd have to fill the emptiness with something else. Sorrow at the prospect of never speaking with him again twisted her heart.

"Oh, Paige. That sounds wonderful. Is there anything I can do to help?"

Paige worked up the energy to chuckle. "Just be there for me. Let's spend time together while I figure out the rest of my life."

"What airline are you flying in on?"

The excitement in her mother's voice eased some of her heartache. It reminded her she had family of her own, and family was worth investing the time and emotional energy.

Paige checked the piece of paper Amy gave her to confirm her reservations and gave her mother the time and flight information. "I should warn you that I have five very large suitcases."

"I can't believe you're finally coming home." Paige heard her mom choke a bit before her voice wobbled. "I'll wait in the cell phone lot. Just text me and I'll meet you at the curb in front of arrivals."

"Okay, see you soon." Paige disconnected the call, a churn of emotions clashing with no clear winner or loser…until she thought of Noah.

She remembered that morning, how he sneaked into the bathroom and made funny faces over her shoulder while she brushed her teeth, and how he made smiley face pancakes for the kids, complete with blueberry eyes and a banana smile.

A tear rolled down her cheek, and she was glad she'd shoved the box of tissues into her backpack, because letting Noah go was going to require the whole box.

And she needed to let him go. She needed to move on.

Her phone buzzed, and Noah's image appeared.

There was no way she was going to answer the phone. She couldn't. He would just talk her into doing something she shouldn't.

She pressed the ignore button and blew her nose. When the phone rang again, she flicked the switch to silent mode, buried the phone in her backpack, and then curled into her seat to watch the sunset.

Thoughts of Noah circled, but she refused to turn them into a negative portrait.

He was truly a wonderful man. Always had been, and always would be.

He just wasn't *her* man.

She watched the sun sink lower and lower in the sky, noting today's display was different. It wasn't the fiery reds and oranges of yesterday. Today was lighter pinks, yellows, and blues. Like the evening colors, more and more disappearing with each passing second, she tucked memories of Noah in a mental box, and when the sun sank down behind the horizon, she shut the box and let the darkness close in.

"Goodbye, Noah Myers. I hope you have a good life."

And just like the airport shuttle, her life moved on.

Chapter 18

*N*oah sat at the table in the dark, a two-finger shot of whisky in front of him. Even if he drank the whole bottle, he wouldn't be able to drink enough to forget the look on Paige's face just before she raced up the steps away from the beach.

The villa was quiet since everyone else was in bed after the long wedding day, but his mind was frantic with unanswered questions. Why did she run off without allowing him to apologize? What was he going to do now? Could she still love him, even with his many flaws?

He blinked when the kitchen light went on. "I figured you wouldn't be able to sleep." Kaylee opened the cabinet to pull out a bag of coffee. "Want some coffee or tea?"

"Neither, tha—" Before he could finish, in walked Julie.

She shrugged out of the fleece jacket she'd put on over her pajamas. "Got any vanilla creamer left?"

"There should be some on the fridge door, second shelf." Kaylee scooped coffee into the basket and then filled the machine with water from the tap.

While Julie bent into the refrigerator looking for the

creamer, his mom appeared. "There's leftover wedding cake if anyone wants a slice."

Kaylee nodded and pulled down some small plates. "Logan's on his way over. Brent volunteered to watch Reece and Ethan."

Noah's gut churned, watching the circling activity. "What's going on?"

Julie turned and gave him a level look. "Mom called a family meeting."

Oh, no. This wasn't good. The last time she called a family meeting, it was two in the morning his time and Logan's ex-wife had just served him with divorce papers. Family meeting meant family intervention. Given the situation with Paige, this intervention was going to be all about him.

Noah tapped his fingers on the glass, wondering whether he should down the shot now, or wait. A minute later, Julie swept the glass away and replaced it with a plate of cake and a cup of coffee. Sugar—his family's solution to all problems.

Julie dropped into the seat next to him. "Are you going to tell us what the note said?"

He didn't have a clue how they all knew about the note. A hotel staff member handed him Paige's message just after he finished giving his wedding toast. He'd tucked the scribbled message in his pocket and hadn't taken it out since. "I can't tell you because I haven't read it."

Kaylee placed extra napkins in the middle of the table. "He's going to ignore it, just like he always does."

"Hey." He waved at Kaylee. "I'm right here. You don't need to talk about me as if I'm three."

"Why not?" Logan asked as he walked into the kitchen and poured a cup of steaming brew. "You act like it sometimes."

"Logan, enough." Mom handed him a plate with a huge

slice of white-frosted cake. "I saved the last piece of lemon-filled because I know it's your favorite."

Noah rolled his eyes. "What are you all doing here?" he asked again, this time hoping for an answer.

Julie pulled the fork out her mouth. "Mom and I were talking about the whole Olivia thing."

"Olivia is not a *thing*. She was a person—a beautiful, caring person who didn't deserve to die." Noah felt the weight of grief hit.

Julie and Mom exchanged a look. "See? Just as I suspected."

Mom held out a hand in warning. "I know you think Noah is remembering a perfect version of Olivia and forgetting all the problems, but that's his issue. Family rule: each of you can only talk about how his leaving after Olivia died impacted you. No pointing fingers. No 'you' statements."

She turned to Logan and invited him to start.

"Me? Why do I have to go first?" He shoved a wedge of cake into his mouth to avoid speaking.

"Because you're still angry." Mom gave Logan her famous squint, warning he was edging toward a scolding.

"Fine. I'm angry." He thunked his plate on the table and spun to face Noah. "You walked away after Olivia died, as if nothing and no one else mattered. I can't even imagine what it was like for you to watch her die and lose all of your dreams and hopes, but damn it, Noah. What about us? What about your family? What about me?" Logan's voice cracked. "After you decided not to go away to college so you could stay here with Olivia and started picking up computer skills, I thought things might not be so bad. Olivia had just started a new therapy regimen that looked promising, and we had plans to start a website design company together. It was the perfect moment to get into the market, but I couldn't make a go of it alone. Within a matter of months, everything fell apart. You just took off. No 'sorry, man.' No nothing. Without a partner, I had to scramble to get a job. If we'd started the company back then, we would have been sitting pretty by now."

"What have you been smoking?" Noah's jaw dropped. "If I remember correctly, you were head over heels in love with Cindy, and she was pressuring you to get a steady job, one with insurance and a retirement plan."

"You see how well that turned out," Logan spat.

"Oh, so now it's my fault your marriage failed?" Noah pushed away from the table, his temper rising.

"Sit," Mom commanded.

"No. I'm not going to sit like a dog." Noah glared at each of his family members. "I'm not responsible for your marriage, Logan, or the fact our family doesn't live ten minutes from each other, Kaylee. We all have our own lives. You want this family back together again, then offer some respect."

"That's what we are trying to do," Julie said softly. "We want to be here for you. We don't want you to be alone tonight."

Oh, hell. He scraped his hair back off his forehead and let out a frustrated breath. Everyone in his family was waiting for him to make a decision—an adult decision. He went with his heart this time, slid back into the chair, and pulled out the piece of paper in his pocket.

He read the note and then passed it to Julie because, of all the people at the table, she wouldn't make a fuss.

Julie read the note, and her eyes searched his. He nodded.

"It's says," Julie held up the piece of paper and read, "'Over the years, you have brought me laughter and joy and friendship. I've truly cherished every moment. I'm just sorry our stars never aligned. I will always love you, and you will always have a piece of my heart to keep forever. Live a good life, Noah. You deserve only the best. Paige.'"

"Aw." Kaylee placed a hand on her heart. "She so loves you, Noah."

"Yeah, and once again, I'm an ass."

"Yes, you are," Logan agreed.

"That's a 'you' statement." Mom frowned in warning. "Keep it up, Logan, and I won't bake my super-secret carrot cake for you ever again. I mean it. Apologize to your brother right now."

Logan shifted in his seat, his eyes not leaving his cake plate. "Sorry, man."

"Try again," Mom ordered. "And mean it this time, because I want Noah to understand something here. He is loved. He is not a failure or a jerk or an ass. He's part of this family, and I didn't raise any defects. I didn't raise any robots either. I raised beautifully fallible, resilient human beings who love and work hard. Each one of you loves the others. What you need to also do is respect each other." She pointed at Noah. "Show your brother respect. Now, before we adjourn this gathering, I want each of you to write down five things you love about Noah."

Noah snorted.

"What?" Julie turned to him. "You don't think I can come up with five?" She crossed her arms. "I can come up with ten." To prove it, she started listing them off.

With each example, the hole in his heart began to stitch shut. Julie didn't stop until she reached twenty to prove her point.

He didn't know what to say. Somehow, there was a difference between thinking someone loved you and knowing they did.

"Do you guys remember when Paige ran out of Olivia's memorial?" He looked around the room.

Kaylee pointed her fork at him. "I remember that, and you ran after her."

"We took a long walk and talked about a lot of things." Noah squeezed his eyes shut for a moment, remembering the pain of the moment. "I realized this morning that, while Olivia is who originally brought us together, Paige and I have our own relationship. A friendship that continued to grow and remain strong despite Olivia no longer being here. That connection has grown into love, except I failed to recognize it. When I called Paige by Olivia's name, it wasn't because I'm still in love with Olivia. It's because Olivia's been on my mind these past few days.

"I see reminders of her everywhere, but it's time to lay those memories to rest. I want to fill my life with new memories, made with Paige. And my family. I'd intended to ask Paige if she wanted to do one of those message-in-a-bottle things together so we could say our final goodbyes to Olivia."

Logan thew his hands up in the air. "Aw, man. Do you have to be better than me at everything? That is just such a perfect explanation. Can't I be better than you at something?" Logan looked at him like he really meant what he said.

"Yo, bro." Noah had a dozen funny things to say but decided now was not the time. "I know one thing you are better at than all of us." Noah did a gut check on his answer and knew it to be true. "You aren't afraid to speak the truth. You don't soft sell anything, and sometimes we need someone we love and trust to help us see the truth. Like when you told me Paige is in love with me and has been for years."

Logan sat back, his chest puffing a bit. "Then let's talk this thing out. How do we get Paige back into the nest, so to speak? I like the idea of her being my sister-in-law, and Flake here seems to really be in love, so what's the plan?"

And just like magic, he was fourteen again, sitting at the table during a family dinner with everyone talking over each other, having side conversations, tossing out some ideas, and rejecting others.

He took a deep breath as he met his mother's gaze. She mouthed, *I love you*, and he returned the gesture.

Sixteen years was a long time to be gone. Too long.

Moving home wasn't the problem. He could have his stuff shipped back. The problem was Paige. He didn't know what she was going to do now. She hadn't answered any of his calls or texts, and he suspected she might run again, like she did last time.

If she did, he wanted to be ready. If she ran, this time he'd go after her and give her five—no, *twenty*—reasons why he loved her and why they needed to find a way to be together.

The only problem was he had to find her first, although he had a good idea where she might have gone.

Just like him, when things got tough, she'd run to family.

Chapter 19

$\mathcal{P}$aige was getting leery of opening her emails, because every morning there were a dozen more job rejections. She sighed. No one seemed to want her unless she had an advanced degree in English, even though she'd been teaching for years.

At least there weren't any emails from Noah. She hadn't heard from him in the week since the wedding. She assumed he'd returned to Singapore to resume his nomadic lifestyle, going back to serial dating, always in search of a woman who could live up to Olivia's iconic perfection. She wasn't prepared to speak to him, but the fact he'd discarded their friendship so easily hurt.

But every day she managed to let go a little more. At the rate she was going, she'd be free of loving Noah in a hundred years or so.

She skimmed down the list of email subject lines and senders, and then noticed Julie's name. She paused. Why would Julie be sending her an email, unless it was related to how she ran out on Mia's wedding? She hesitated, took a deep breath, then opened the message.

"Carmen" the email began, "I'd like to introduce you to Paige Weaver. She's the woman I told you about. She was great when counseling our daughter, Charley, about her interest in studying abroad in Costa Rica. Paige has taught English as a Foreign Language for years, has traveled extensively, and is amazing with young people. She understands the ins and outs of students trying to get into the US college system, as well as into overseas programs. I think she would be perfect for your open International Student Strategist position."

Paige stared at the screen. The TEFL community was very tight-knit, and friends helped friends find jobs all the time, but she never thought help would come from the Myers family, especially after she disappeared without a word.

She scanned her email with mounting excitement, backtracking to an email from Carmen Santos. She opened it and read: "Hi, Paige. A mutual friend passed along your name and credentials, and you sound like a good match for a position we currently have open out of our Oakland office. It's a work-from-home position with weekly in-office meetings. I'm including a link with more information about the job. If you think you might be interested, contact me to set up an interview."

Paige clicked on the website link and found a beautifully designed, full-page spread. The pictures of young people were vibrant and fun. The job description detailed a position that provided one-on-one counseling and support for international students who wanted to study in the US. She loved the idea of helping to coordinate college tours and going through the selection process with young adults. She knew the importance many cultures placed on education, and the huge investment families made to provide a college degree for their children.

The more she delved into the website, the more excited she got. This consulting company was one of the top-rated agencies in the country. She even liked the list of essay prompts developed to give students a place to start, and the blog showed the agency was involved with students as early as high school.

By the time she finished reading every page on the site and researching Carmen's LinkedIn page, she was ready for an initial phone call.

She picked up her phone and dialed the number, overflowing with buoyant enthusiasm. "Hello, may I please speak with Carmen Santos? My name is Paige Weaver."

"Just one moment," a perky female voice responded. "Let me transfer the call."

Seconds later Paige heard a feminine, "Hello?"

Carmen's brisk, friendly voice fit the image Paige had constructed after reading her profile. Carmen Santos appeared to be a go-getter, first working at Yale, Harvard, and a Wall Street financial firm before launching her own company, which was now international. She was a woman on fire, and Paige liked that passion.

"Hi, Carmen. This is Paige Weaver. I was referred to you by a mutual acquaintance, Julie Myers…oops, Keyning. I met her long before she was married."

"Oh, yes. I'm glad to hear from you. Did you have an opportunity to research the position we're currently recruiting for?"

"I did." Goose bumps rose on her arms as a happy premonition hit. This was the perfect opportunity she'd been hoping for. "I'd love to learn more about the job, and I'm already impressed by what I've learned about your agency. The results list is impressive, as are your sponsors, and you have some mighty big names backing you. You must be so proud of what you've built."

"Thank you, Paige. I see you really have done your homework." Paige could hear papers rustling in the background. "When can we do a video interview? I'd like you to meet with both our domestic and international advisor leads."

"That sounds great, but I want to be up front, Carmen. I don't have a degree yet. My goal is to work full-time and enroll in online classes while working towards a master's."

"We can discuss the details during your interview. Do you speak any foreign languages?"

"Yes. I'm fluent in Spanish, and can have a conversation in French. I've been studying Mandarin, but not quite fluid yet."

"Again, I'm impressed. You bring valuable assets to the table as a candidate. Are you available tomorrow?" Carmen asked.

Excitement ping-ponged through her, making her giddy.

She and her mother had made plans to spend the day together, complete with mani-pedis, lunch, and shopping. It was the first step in getting to know each other again. Her excitement dimmed. "I'm sorry, Carmen, I already have commitments tomorrow."

"Not to worry. How about Friday?"

Paige's joy came bouncing back. "Friday would be great."

"You're now on my calendar. I'll have my assistant schedule a group video interview and send you additional information about the position," Carmen said.

"Sounds good. See you then." Paige punctuated her reply with an enthusiastic fist pump and disconnected the call, dancing into the kitchen where her mom was making breakfast.

Her mom set a mug on the table, dropped into a chair, and Paige got a whiff of her favorite Chai tea blend.

"It sounds like you have an interview." Her mom swiped

butter across a slice of toast and added it to the stack on a small plate.

"I do." Paige reached for her cup. "Thanks for the tea. It's my favorite."

The warm vanilla cream with the underlying notes of orange, nutmeg, clove, and cinnamon reminded her of the lush green tea hills in the Phu Tho province, a place not far from Hanoi, a short trip she liked to take to get out of the city. The area had several temples, pagodas, and shrines cradled in the mountains and lowland plains, and its scenic charm made it one of her favorite places to visit—the keyword being visit.

Although her mom had relocated from Oakland to Los Angeles after Olivia's death, just being with her felt like home. She still wore her hair in a short bob and favored capris and tunic tops. Breakfast was scrambled eggs and toast, lunch would be tuna salad, and dinner would be some type of grilled fish and sautéed veggies. The predictability drove Paige insane as a teenager, but now she found it comforting.

"Tell me about the call," her mom said while pouring a glass of juice.

Paige took a long sip, savoring the spices, mind whirling with possibilities. "I have a good feeling about this one." She told her mom about the call and what she learned. "I'm surprised Julie recommended me."

"I'm not. The Myers family isn't like that. They don't hold grudges or judge people. If anything, they're amazingly understanding of the decisions people make in difficult situations. Mrs. Myers is one of the few people I could talk to about Olivia and the divorce and my regrets after you went to Europe." Her mom set a plate mounded with yumminess in front of her. "We still talk every once in a while, and I've run into Mia at the hospital where I volunteer a couple of times."

Paige was startled. She assumed her mother had cut ties with everyone who reminded her of Olivia. But having experienced Bernice Myers's kindness for herself during the wedding weekend, she shouldn't be surprised. All the Myers family members had made an effort to help her feel included.

"Oh, I've been meaning to give this to you all week. I finally dug it out of a bin in the back of my closet." Her mom scooted a brown cardboard box across the table. Faded pink and red hearts were glued to the top, along with a patchy dusting of sparkles.

"I remember this." Paige lifted the lid to see a feather, a rock, some letters and photos, and other trinkets. She lifted Noah's high school graduation picture to read the back.

Hey, Squirt. Something to remember me. Noah

There was a picture of her dad and mom, arms around each other's waists, in front of a giant redwood tree, and another photo of her mom and her standing together in the garden with Tiger, Olivia's cat, peeking out from under a bush in the background.

She picked up a football pin that once belonged to Noah. After high school, he didn't want it anymore and gave it to Paige when she asked. There was also a CD of NSYNC's fourth album, *Celebrity*, which Noah gave her for Christmas when she was fourteen. In the bottom was her diary, a small journal covered with purple fabric, its gold-plated lock broken long ago.

She flipped through the worn pages until one entry caught her eye. It was a poem to Noah about how she wished he could see her love. The next several pages were about her dreams of getting married and living happily ever after with Noah. She choked off a sob. Those were childhood dreams, not reality.

She put the book aside, unable to read any more entries. They reminded her that she was still clinging to childish hopes.

Her mom picked up the journal but didn't open it. "Sometimes it's so hard to look back. It's painful to remember. But sometimes the only thing bringing me comfort is remembering. Are you still in love with Noah, honey?"

Paige's head jerked up. Obviously, she hadn't done a very good job of hiding her feelings. She thought she'd hidden her secret from everyone, including Olivia and her parents. Spending time with the Myers, however, revealed that her love wasn't the best-kept-secret.

"How did you know?" she asked her mother.

"It's impossible to hide something like that, Paige. When you were young, I thought you'd outgrow your crush. It's not uncommon for younger sisters to idolize their older sisters' boyfriends."

"He was nice to me. Someone I could talk too. I don't want to hurt you, but you were always so busy taking care of Olivia."

Her mom's smile was sad. "We never meant to favor Olivia over you, but the cancer dominated all our lives, even yours. That's not an excuse, but an acknowledgement. What makes you so truly special, Paige, is you never seemed to resent Olivia for it. You were the perfect little sister."

Paige leaned back in her chair. "I think that was the problem. I succeeded at being perfect to the point that no one saw me anymore."

Her mom sighed. "Sometimes I wonder how things would have turned out if Olivia hadn't gotten sick the second time. One thing I feel certain of, is she and Noah wouldn't have married. Those two were never suited for the long haul.

Your father tried talking Noah out of it, but Noah was determined."

A tingle of surprise raced up her spine. "I could have told dad not to bother. Once Noah sets his mind on something, he doesn't let go."

"He can be rather focused." Her mom took a sip from her own mug. "Does he know you love him?"

The question slammed into her like a bowling ball hitting a strike. Good thing she was already sitting down. She considered hedging, but then decided not to bother. The truth was coming out, and there was no reason to deny it to her mother.

"We talked about the possibility of a relationship at Mia's wedding. He knows how I feel, but he's still stuck on Olivia." Paige shrugged. "But it was always a big maybe. My love isn't enough for him to let go and take a chance." She looked out the window of her mom's townhome at the clear blue slice of sky. "I'll always love Noah. I gave him my heart a long time ago, and I've never found anyone else I want to share myself with. The truth is, I always hoped…"

"Hope is a good starting place, but it doesn't get the job done. Sometimes you have to face your fears and jump in with both feet." Her mom glanced at the wall clock and stood to clear the table, the food barely touched.

Paige pointed to her not-yet-empty plate. "Cleaning up already? Do you have somewhere to be?" she asked, mentally reviewing her own lack of plans for the day. She'd planned to research more job leads, but the interview with Carmen was promising enough that the urgency driving her faded.

The rumble of a car engine sounded from behind the townhome and then cut off.

"Right on time." Her mother pulled back the sheer white curtain and gave a confirming nod.

Paige looked at her mother when she heard a car door close. "Are you expecting company?"

Her mother studied her with caring eyes. "Sometimes, Paige, we do and say things we regret. Sometimes we need to be given a second chance. You gave me one when I didn't deserve it, and I hope you have one more to give."

"Mom." Paige's whole body sagged with dread. "What have you done?"

"I want you to have what you've always wanted." She pointed to the journal, then strode to the back door. "I invited Noah here, but it's up to you whether you choose to give Noah a second chance or not."

Paige sat unmoving. Stunned, frightened, thrilled.

"Hey, Mrs. Weaver. Thanks for giving me a call."

The sound of Noah's warm, husky baritone triggered a full-body reaction. Her pulse sped up, her skin prickled, her belly clenched, and her palms got clammy.

She wanted to berate her mother for forcing her into this confrontation...and hug her for arranging a second chance after her own courage failed. A tiny sob choked her as she remembered what moms were for.

The eggs and toast sat in her stomach like a rock. She forced herself to stand, rising to her feet just as Noah entered the sunny yellow-and-white kitchen.

He looked more delicious than a New York cheesecake with sweet cherries and chocolate drizzled on top.

His olive-green cargo pants hung on his hips just right, and he was wearing a white T-shirt and white tennis shoes. To top it off, he held a bouquet of red tulips, because he already knew roses weren't her favorite.

"What are you doing here, Noah?"

"I came to apologize." The lines radiating from the corners of his dark eyes showed he was just as anxious about seeing her as she was him.

She crossed her arms, shoulders hunched as if to protect her heart. "You've apologized before."

"I'm not perfect, Paige." He held her gaze with eyes that burned with sincerity. "This isn't the last mistake I'll ever make, or my final apology. These past few weeks, I've confronted some painful truths about myself and uncovered feelings I never acknowledged. I'm changing, or at least trying to change, and I know I won't get it right straight out of the gate. If you love me the way you said you did, don't I at least deserve an opportunity to say what I came here to tell you?"

She shuddered hearing him use her admission of love as justification to force her into listening to his apology. "For the record, my feelings haven't changed, Noah, but I learned some painful lessons myself this weekend. Love isn't enough. Love didn't keep Olivia alive. It didn't save my parents' marriage. And it didn't keep either of us here after she died, even though we had the love of our families." She lifted her chin, feigning courage. "But I still care enough to hear what you have to say."

"Okay. That's good. Really good." He set the flowers on the table and inched closer to her. "Here's the thing. I didn't mean to hurt you. Calling you Olivia was an accident. Still, I know I hurt you. I think you believe I called you Olivia because I still want her, or see her, instead of you. That's not true."

She backed away as he drew closer, desperate to maintain the distance so she could think straight.

"I'm sad Olivia died. That part of my life—our life—is over. And I'm ready to stop running. It's time to put the past to rest and look ahead to the future. But I can't reach for the future without you. There are big changes ahead. For both of us."

She gasped not sure what he meant. "What kind of changes?"

"I'm going to be a better uncle and brother. More present. More involved."

"What does better entail?" She wasn't ready to grasp at hope yet. She needed to know more.

"Logan and I are going into business together." He glanced down at the floor, then back up. "I'm moving back to Oakland. Settling down. Buying a house. Showing up at Mom's for family dinners every Sunday."

"Why?" She barely squeezed out the word. Was it for himself? His family? Or her?

"I'm tired of always being on the move. I miss my family. I miss belonging." He gazed deep into her eyes. "I'm tired of running and still hurting. Carrying all of this emotional baggage is exhausting. Don't you think?"

Noah was putting all her feelings into his words. She was tired. She was lonely. She'd been around the world, seeking peace and solace and never finding it. There was only one more place to look, and that was the place she'd left sixteen years ago.

"We've wasted so much time." He closed the distance between them and circled his arms around her, so her cheek rested against his chest. "After Olivia died, I went looking for something or someone to fill the empty space in my heart. Not as a replacement for Olivia, but to fill my life with love and laughter and joy and purpose. I was blind, or maybe too afraid, to see you were everything I needed. I may not have said it, but I've always seen you, Paige. You, and everything that makes you an amazing woman."

"I felt bad for wanting you. You belonged to Olivia." She closed her eyes to hide the tears, but they wet his shirt anyway. "I couldn't help loving you, Noah. If she was still alive—"

"We need to stop second-guessing ourselves and playing the what-if game. Olivia is gone. I loved her then, but I love you now. For the rest of our days together, I will love you, Paige."

"But—"

He silenced her with a tender, passionate kiss. "Love might not be enough, Paige, but trust and respect are everything. It's what gives us courage and hope and strength. It's what finally brought us together."

Chapter 20

"This was a good choice." Paige stood on a rugged bluff overlooking the Pacific Ocean.

It was just after six a.m. and the water was still inky, but streaks of vibrant orange and gold and red announced daybreak. This early they were the only visitors at Point Fermin Park, but she was grateful for the solitude. She wanted this moment to be private and special, shared only with Noah.

"Mia suggested this place. She said when the view is clear, you can see all up the coast all the way to Santa Catalina Island." Noah stood next to her, a slight gap between them.

Paige wasn't bothered by the lack of contact. They'd come here together to say their farewells to Olivia, but their goodbyes were a task to be completed alone.

Without another word, Noah shrugged out of his backpack and held the black bag out to her by the straps. Paige unzipped the bag and pulled out two bottles. He dropped the backpack, the faint scrape of fabric against the dirt the only sound besides the hushed murmur of the waves on the rocks below.

She handed him the dark green bottle, swallowing when emotion tightened her throat. It was the champagne bottle from Olivia and Noah's wedding. Her mother had held onto the keepsake, but when they told her about their plans, she offered the saved wedding token to Noah.

Paige's letter to Olivia was sealed in a clear soda bottle imprinted with a white label reading NEHI Orange. The sweet, sugary beverage was a rare summertime treat when they were growing up, and Paige couldn't count how many times her sister soothed a hurt or brightened a rough day by surprising Paige with a bottle from the corner store.

She closed her eyes and inhaled the brisk, salty air. She concentrated on the rough ground beneath her feet and the teasing caress of a tendril of hair across her cheek as the gentle morning breeze made it dance. She listened to the sound of Noah's rhythmic breathing and rested her hand on her chest so she could feel the steady beat of her heart. She felt the burn of tears and let them come. She let the emotions ripple through her, accepting and acknowledging each wave: the heavy weight of grief, the butterfly lightness of hope, and the healing warmth of peace.

She wanted to remember this moment. To be *in* this moment. Just like she wanted to savor every minute going forward.

Olivia's death had robbed Paige, her parents, Noah, his family, and their friends of so much. But thanks to the group, she was learning to recognize the loss didn't only take. It gave, but sometimes people weren't ready to accept those gifts.

Losing Olivia taught Paige the value of family and the importance of nurturing those relationships. It taught her to be strong and resilient, kind and compassionate. It prompted her to venture out into the world and discover potentials in herself that she'd never imagined.

Learning to receive affection also gave her the gift of Noah's love.

Noah's love was the greatest treasure of all, and she acknowledged the love in her letter to her sister, which read...

Dear Olivia~

I miss you every single day. It's been sixteen years, but you are still an important part of my life. There's so much I wish I could share with you. I believe you know how I feel, wherever you are, but it's not the same as sitting on the pier and sharing a Nehi or ice cream cone. Now we're both grown up, we'd probably be sharing a bottle of wine.

Life isn't fair, but you probably know that better than anyone. So much of your time was spent in hospitals or in pain, and I'm glad, truly glad, you are no longer suffering. You were, and still are, loved by so many. Mom and Dad would do anything for you. I adore you. Plus, Noah gave you his whole heart and soul.

At least, that's what I thought until recently.

I often wonder if you knew how I felt about Noah, and what a bittersweet moment your marriage was for me. If anyone deserved to be loved by a man like Noah, it was you, but I couldn't help but be a little jealous. I can admit that now. I was jealous...still am, a little.

So many things changed after you died.

Until now, I believed I was running away from the grief of losing you. That was a big part of why I left home, but there was another reason.

Yeah, Noah.

I felt guilty because he and I were still here when you were gone. And even if he did, by some miracle, learn to care for me, what kind of woman took her sister's husband?

For the longest time, I didn't have to worry about that. Noah and I were friends, survivors connected by our love for you, plus he'd vowed to love you forever.

I learned so many painful lessons losing you. But recently I discovered something joyful. Our hearts aren't limited in their capacity to love. There's plenty to go around for everyone. Noah can love both of us. You are his past love, and I'm his future love.

If there is anyone I'm willing to share this man's love with, it's you, sis.

Thank you, Olivia. You're the world's best big sister, and I cherish every moment we had together.

Love you always,
Paige

She hadn't shared her letter with Noah, nor asked him to reveal what he'd written in his. Since the day he showed up at her mother's townhome with that creative, heartfelt apology, they'd talked. Really talked. Confessed fears. Revealed hopes. Confided secrets. Expressed feelings.

They still hadn't found the perfect solution for moving forward, but they were closer to making it happen. As frightening as it was to bare her soul to Noah, Paige discovered negotiating a relationship and learning to compromise and problem-solve together was exhilarating. Every conversation, every touch, every kiss assured her he was just as committed to their newly formed relationship as she was.

He saw her.

He understood her.

Noah loved her.

"Ready?" she whispered.

"Yes."

Noah stepped closer to the edge of the bluff first. He pressed a kiss to the bottle, which glinted momentarily in a single ray of morning sun, and then drew his arm back to fling the champagne bottle over the cliff, watching as it tumbled through the air and disappeared into the surf.

He slowly swung around to face her, palming the tears off his cheek. "Your turn."

For a second Paige felt light-headed, as if she was in a dream. She actually felt Olivia's presence, and a warm sensation of approval and affection filled her. It was the same thing she felt when she was young and Olivia focused all her attention on Paige. The brilliant flash of love and connection when Paige knew Olivia *saw* her.

She mimicked Noah's action, hurling the Nehi bottle into the air, only to watch it fall into the water below.

Paige felt Noah come up behind her, wrapping his arms around her waist. She leaned back against him, surrounded by his strength and love. She knew Olivia understood she never intended to steal Noah's heart.

There was enough love for everyone—those who were in their lives now, those who'd passed, and those still to come.

Chapter 21

*T*wo days later, Noah changed the rental car stereo to the playlist on his phone. He tightened his grip on the steering wheel, navigating through a familiar Oakland neighborhood, nervous about what he was going to reveal to Paige. For the first time in sixteen years, he was scared he might again lose his girl. Only the stakes were higher this time. This time the possibility of forever truly existed.

Paige was healthy, had her entire life ahead of her, and could go anywhere in the world she wanted.

He just wanted her to stay with him.

He glanced over to see Paige rocking out to the first song on the playlist, a boy band pop song popular when they were teenagers. "I love this song." She snapped her fingers and wiggled in her seat next to him.

Suddenly, she paused and looked at him as the next tune started. It was "Girlfriend", from NSYNC's *Celebrity* album. "This isn't the radio, is it?"

He exhaled. She noticed. Just like always. She noticed when he was excited, sad, or frustrated. He was working hard to do the same.

Paige leaned forward, looking down the side street when he paused at a stop sign. "I know where we are. This is close to where we grew up. Don't Kaylee and John live around here?"

"Close. They live about two miles east." He pointed to his right. "And Logan lives about five miles that way." He pointed south. He thumbed a quick text message and placed his phone in the middle console.

Ten minutes later Noah turned down a narrow street with houses on both sides. Each was small, but well maintained. He pulled up in front of a modest, one-story gray home with white trim and an eye-catching red door with a For Lease sign stuck in the front lawn. He parked the car at the curb and shut off the engine.

"Come on." He took a deep breath and opened the car door.

"Is this what you want to show me?" She looked at him with raised brows.

He expected her skepticism. It was the same when Kaylee showed him the place earlier in the week. He knew Kaylee had a passion for decorating, but had no idea she and John had started investing in properties and flipping or renting, depending on the market conditions.

He pulled out the keys and waited for Paige to join him on the sidewalk.

"What's going on?" She looked up and down the street.

"You'll see." He unlocked the front door and let her walk inside first.

The single-family home was small, the design typical of a home built in the sixties, with newly polished hardwood floors and freshly painted walls in a modern shade of light cream.

He guided her through the empty rooms to the kitchen, where a small table had been set for two with fresh flowers and candles to create a romantic setting. The tempting aroma of something garlicky and tomatoey filled the air.

"Did you just call Kaylee?" she asked.

"Yes. I texted her just a few minutes ago."

Paige looked around the kitchen. "I don't understand."

He tapped his fingers on the tiled counter, his fear hiking up a notch. "I had a long talk with my siblings the night you left. It wasn't pleasant, and at one point I thought Logan might punch me again."

Her mouth opened like she was about to say something, but he waved off her concern. " Don't worry. Mom played referee. And I was okay. The bottom line is the family wants me to come home."

"Why didn't they just say so in the first place?"

He chuckled. Oh, he so loved this woman. "My thought exactly." He lifted her hand in his. "Their biggest concern was that I might get on the next plane home. I knew I hurt you, and I felt terrible."

"Maybe I was looking to be hurt, just waiting for an excuse to convince myself you could never love me." She looked at him with steady eyes, the quick flash of pain replaced with love. "It's easy to say you love someone, but putting the feelings into action is harder. It means trusting them, forgiving them, being vulnerable. Walking away is so much easier. Staying is a lot riskier."

"But think of the payoff," he whispered, brushing his knuckles over the curve of her cheek.

During the two days they spent together in LA, they'd done a lot of talking. They agreed that honesty, no matter how difficult, was the best policy. Being open was the only way to avoid misunderstandings and flawed assumptions.

"But I'm not the only one they want to come home. They want you to come back as well."

Her eyes searched his. "Is that why Julie recommended me for the counseling job?"

"No," he hedged. "I mean, yes, sort of. Julie wouldn't have recommended you if she didn't feel you were more than qualified for the job, but she did have an ulterior motive. She wants you here, as part of the Myers family."

"Noah, I—"

"Wait. Before you say anything, I want to show you something." He tugged on her hand, pulling her out of the kitchen to the front room. He walked into a bright, sunlit room with a large window looking out at the street and the front sidewalk. "Over here, I picture my desk, and over here, your desk. If one of us is on the phone, the other can work in the living room or kitchen."

Paige looked around the space and then turned to him. "I—"

"Wait. There's more." He grabbed her hand. "And here's the most special room."

She looked at the wood floor extending from kitchen to bedroom, and the cream-colored walls that somehow gave the flooring extra richness and texture.

The only difference was the en suite bathroom, but that wasn't what he meant by special. He escorted her to the middle of the room.

"This"—he opened his arms wide to estimate the size of a queen-sized bed—"is where I want to make love to you. I want to hold you in my arms every night and tell you funny stories until you fall asleep in my arms. I want to spend the rest of my life with you, and make up for the time we've lost."

"Are you asking me to move in with you?" Her face fell.

"I'm asking you to be part of me. Part of my family." He took her into his arms. "I want to marry you, Paige. We've lost so many years together. But this feels right. I rushed into marriage with Olivia, Okay. Yes. But I know we don't have forever. I want us to celebrate every milestone in our relationship. When the time is right to marry, we'll celebrate with all the important people in our lives."

She walked to the window, gazing out over the small garden area, where she stood quietly for the longest time.

"Before you answer, I have one more thing to show you."

He raced to the door and beckoned to her to follow him, hoping beyond hope that he'd gotten all the right stuff. As she walked down the back porch steps, he hurried round the corner and was relieved to find Kaylee had arranged everything perfectly.

He pointed at the metal and wood garden bench, complete with trowel, shears, and pots with mint, thyme, and rosemary.

She lifted a sprig of rosemary, rubbing her fingers together, and brought her fingertips to her nose.

"Olivia hated gardening." She rested her hand on the thick, wooden planter's block. "She hated bees and worms and dirt."

He caught the choked-off emotion and slid his arms around her waist. "I know."

"She was into makeup and fashion." She finally relaxed into his arms.

"And every summer you and your dad would plant lettuce, cucumbers, and beets. And when you were sixteen, you got upset because a rabbit got into the yard and pulled up all your plants and gnawed on the plant spikes you hand-painted to show what was planted where."

She sniffed and rubbed at her nose. "She also hated playing video games."

"Thus the reason you and I always played when I came over." His arms tightened around her waist. "I don't know why it took me so long to figure out we were always meant to be together."

"You see me," she said, the words so low he almost didn't hear them. "You see me now."

"Yes, Paige. I always saw you, but sometimes we have to reframe how we're seeing it." He stiffened. "Oh, crap. I forgot our dinner is in the oven. Kaylee's going to kill me. She made lasagna because my cooking sucks."

He sprinted up the steps, laughing when Paige yelled, "I know."

He pulled the pan out of the oven, hoping it wasn't over-baked. "I think it'll be okay."

"I know it'll be okay." She'd followed him back into the house. Something in her tone had changed, and she came to him, wrapping an arm around his waist.

"So, what do you say? Kaylee says we can buy the house if we want."

"It looks like the perfect place for us. If Carmen offers me the job, I can apply to Berkeley. I'm hoping to get accepted into their teaching program."

"You want to go back to school?"

"Yeah, I do. Along the way, I found out I'm a really good teacher. One day I'd like to have my doctorate."

"That would be awesome. I can already imagine your certificate hanging on the wall." He pulled her in closer.

"Before I say yes, there's one more thing." She smoothed a wave of hair off his forehead.

She did that nervous bite-the-lip thing, so he knew this was big. "What is it?"

"I didn't tell you—I didn't even tell my mom—but I had a breast cancer scare a few years ago. They caught it early, and I didn't even need chemo. But there's always a chance it could come back. If it does—"

"—then we will face it together. You and I."

"I don't want you to feel obligated. I know how hard it was to watch Olivia fade away."

"It wasn't easy. But this situation is entirely different." He waited until her eyes met his. "This time, I won't be staying because I have some fallible notion that I can save your life. I learned that lesson. If the cancer happens to come back, I will be here, not because of the cancer, but because I love you, and I want to be here for you."

"So you're not scared?"

"Oh, I'm scared." He cradled her hand against his chest. "But as long as you can feel my heart beating, I will love you. Cancer or no cancer."

She reached up and cupped his jaw in her palm. "It took us long enough to get here."

"But we are here. That's what counts. I love you, Paige."

"I love you, too, Noah."

Fireworks exploded in his body, sizzling out to his extremities.

"You never got to hear my toast at the wedding. How about some champagne?" He took a bottle of the champagne the vintner at Silver Fox had recommended out of the refrigerator. When he twisted off the cork, a fountain of bubbles exploded from the top, and he rushed for the sink.

Paige grabbed the flutes from the table and he poured the bubbly, his anxiety returning as he handed her one of the glasses. He raised his in a toast. "To us."

She held up her glass and paused. "What's this?"

She stared at the ring in the bottom of the champagne flute.

"Marry me, Paige. Not today, but soon. Help me be the man I want to be for you."

She set the glass on the counter and slid her arms around his neck. "It's about time you got around to that question."

"Is that a yes?"

"Well, I don't know," she teased, eyes shining. "Of course,

it's a yes! In fact, it's a double, triple, quadruple yes." She kissed his cheek, nose, chin. "Yes! Yes! Yes!"

Then she grabbed her champagne glass and guzzled the contents to get to the ring.

She gave the beveled diamond ring back to him, the one he agonized over for hours, hoping she would like it. In the end, he chose this design because of its simplicity. She could garden, work with kids, sew, or make love with him without having to worry about losing the diamond. But if she lost the ring…oh, well. He would still have her.

He held out the gold circle embedded with diamonds so she could slip her finger into it. "Do you like it?"

She cupped his face again and gave him a great, big, smacking kiss. "I love it. It's perfect, just like you."

And, just like that, he was home, because no matter where he went, Paige would always be the place he came back to.

I'm so glad you could join Paige and Noah on their journey to their happily ever after.

Do you want to read another Silver Fox Resort Novel?

Sweet December, a limited edition release, is included in the *Holiday Fake Out* box set, but you must hurry to get this special release for 99¢.

Those of you who have read my books or been part of my newsletter have heard my explanation for why Authors never see their Star Ratings requested by Amazon, so thank you for allowing me to share the information once again.

When Amazon asks a reader to "Rate this book" on their Kindle, Amazon is the only one to see these ratings.

I'm left clueless about how you feel about this book. Your input matters.

Book reviews help me decide what kind of books I write. Plus, the more people who leave a review, the more likely Amazon is to move a book up in the rankings? Written reviews help other readers find and love a series.

Please continue to rate the book on your Kindle or reader as this helps Amazon, but take an extra moment to pop over to the review section and leave a few words!

Seriously, a few words like, "great story," is enough.

If you have not read my Elkridge Series or the Lonely Ridge Collection, and have no idea why authors keep asking you as a reader to take a few minutes to leave even a couple of word reviews, here's the break down of how reviews work in this crazy business.

Reviews (not ratings) help authors qualify for advertising opportunities. Without triple digit reviews, an author may miss out on these valuable opportunities. And with only a "star rating" the author has little chance of participating in specific promotions, which means authors continue to struggle, and many talented writers give up writing altogether.

Readers aren't the only ones who use reviews to help make purchasing decisions. Producers and directors use your reviews when looking for new projects.

This is why I'm asking for your help.

A few kind words make such a massive difference to me. Your words give me the encouragement I need to continue writing because honestly, I write my books for you, and I'd like to keep delivering the types of stories you want to read.

And, yes, every book in a series needs reviews, not just the first book. Even if a book has been out for awhile, a fresh review can breathe new life into a book.

So, please take a few minutes to leave a short review. Even a couple of words will brighten my day.

Lastly. Thank you for reading this book. I hope to see you again soon. Cheers!

More Books By
Lyz Kelley

SILVER FOX RESORT
SILVER SPOON
SILVER DOLLAR
SILVER BELLS
SWEET CHAMPAGNE
SWEET CHARDONNAY

SECRETS
BILLIONAIRE'S SECRET
DOCTOR'S SECRET

THE ELKRIDGE SERIES
BLINDED
ABANDONED
ORPHANED
RESCUED
UNMISTAKEN
ATONEMENT
BITTERSWEET
Coming soon:
GUARDED

Do you want a free book?

I've got a present for my readers, your very own ebook exclusive.

https://geni.us/LyzKelleyFreeBook

Sign up to start falling in love today!

Acknowledgments

for Sweet Champagne

For years, I've wanted to help junior authors hone their craft without the worry of having to publish or put their name out into the market place before they were ready. Then an idea came to me, what if I created a story outline, then worked with these deserving authors to write a book?

Well, you can probably guess where this is going, this story is a product of one of those collaborations.

So to all those who took part and worked on this book, you know who you are, you all have my sincere gratitude for taking this wonderful journey with me.

~ Lyz

Thank you for reading: SWEET
CHAMPAGNE

Award-winning author Lyz Kelley mixes a little bit of heart, healing, humanity, happiness, honor, hope, and honor in all her books that are written especially for you.

She's is a total disaster in the kitchen, a compulsive neat freak, a tea snob, and adores writing about and falling in love with everyday heroes.

Please also consider leaving a review on Amazon Goodreads and/or BookBub. Reviews help readers find new books to read, and authors find their footing.

You can also find Lyz on Facebook and Instagram for news, contests, giveaways, and more exciting stuff!

Belvitri
Services

Copyright

or are used fictitiously, and any resemblance to the actual persons, living or dead, business establishments, events or locales is entirely coincidental. For questions and comments about the quality of this book please contact us at Lyz Kelley's contact page.

Cover Art: Covers by Megan Parker

Made in the USA
Monee, IL
20 January 2022